TO ENDANGER LIVES

DI SAM COBBS
BOOK NINE

M A COMLEY

Copyright © 2023 by M A Comley

All rights reserved.

No part of this book may be reproduced in any form or by any electronic or mechanical means, including information storage and retrieval systems, without written permission from the author, except for the use of brief quotations in a book review.

Thank you once again to Clive Rowlandson for allowing me to use one of his stunning photos for the cover.

ACKNOWLEDGMENTS

Special thanks as always go to @studioenp for their superb cover design expertise.

My heartfelt thanks go to my wonderful editor Emmy, and my proofreader Joseph for spotting all the lingering nits.

Thank you also to my amazing ARC Group who help to keep me sane during this process.

Thank you also to Jean Roberts for allowing me to use her name as a character in this novel.

To Mary, gone, but never forgotten. I hope you found the peace you were searching for my dear friend. I miss you each and every day.

ALSO BY M A COMLEY

Blind Justice (Novella)
Cruel Justice (Book #1)
Mortal Justice (Novella)
Impeding Justice (Book #2)
Final Justice (Book #3)
Foul Justice (Book #4)
Guaranteed Justice (Book #5)
Ultimate Justice (Book #6)
Virtual Justice (Book #7)
Hostile Justice (Book #8)
Tortured Justice (Book #9)
Rough Justice (Book #10)
Dubious Justice (Book #11)
Calculated Justice (Book #12)
Twisted Justice (Book #13)
Justice at Christmas (Short Story)
Prime Justice (Book #14)
Heroic Justice (Book #15)
Shameful Justice (Book #16)
Immoral Justice (Book #17)
Toxic Justice (Book #18)
Overdue Justice (Book #19)
Unfair Justice (a 10,000 word short story)
Irrational Justice (a 10,000 word short story)

Seeking Justice (a 15,000 word novella)

Caring For Justice (a 24,000 word novella)

Savage Justice (a 17,000 word novella)

Justice at Christmas #2 (a 15,000 word novella)

Gone in Seconds (Justice Again series #1)

Ultimate Dilemma (Justice Again series #2)

Shot of Silence (Justice Again series #3)

Taste of Fury (Justice Again series #4)

Crying Shame (Justice Again series #5)

See No Evil (Justice Again #6)

To Die For (DI Sam Cobbs #1)

To Silence Them (DI Sam Cobbs #2)

To Make Them Pay (DI Sam Cobbs #3)

To Prove Fatal (DI Sam Cobbs #4)

To Condemn Them (DI Sam Cobbs #5)

To Punish Them (DI Sam Cobbs #6)

To Entice Them (DI Sam Cobbs #7)

To Control Them (DI Sam Cobbs #8)

To Endanger Lives (DI Sam Cobbs #9)

Forever Watching You (DI Miranda Carr thriller)

Wrong Place (DI Sally Parker thriller #1)

No Hiding Place (DI Sally Parker thriller #2)

Cold Case (DI Sally Parker thriller #3)

Deadly Encounter (DI Sally Parker thriller #4)

Lost Innocence (DI Sally Parker thriller #5)

Goodbye My Precious Child (DI Sally Parker #6)

The Missing Wife (DI Sally Parker #7)

Truth or Dare (DI Sally Parker #8)

Where Did She Go? (DI Sally Parker #9)

Web of Deceit (DI Sally Parker Novella with Tara Lyons)

The Missing Children (DI Kayli Bright #1)

Killer On The Run (DI Kayli Bright #2)

Hidden Agenda (DI Kayli Bright #3)

Murderous Betrayal (Kayli Bright #4)

Dying Breath (Kayli Bright #5)

Taken (DI Kayli Bright #6)

The Hostage Takers (DI Kayli Bright Novella)

No Right to Kill (DI Sara Ramsey #1)

Killer Blow (DI Sara Ramsey #2)

The Dead Can't Speak (DI Sara Ramsey #3)

Deluded (DI Sara Ramsey #4)

The Murder Pact (DI Sara Ramsey #5)

Twisted Revenge (DI Sara Ramsey #6)

The Lies She Told (DI Sara Ramsey #7)

For The Love Of… (DI Sara Ramsey #8)

Run for Your Life (DI Sara Ramsey #9)

Cold Mercy (DI Sara Ramsey #10)

Sign of Evil (DI Sara Ramsey #11)

Indefensible (DI Sara Ramsey #12)

Locked Away (DI Sara Ramsey #13)

I Can See You (DI Sara Ramsey #14)

The Kill List (DI Sara Ramsey #15)

Crossing The Line (DI Sara Ramsey #16)

Time to Kill (DI Sara Ramsey #17)

Deadly Passion (DI Sara Ramsey #18)

Son Of The Dead (DI Sara Ramsey #19)

Evil Intent (DI Sara Ramsey #20)

I Know The Truth (A Psychological thriller)

She's Gone (A psychological thriller)

Shattered Lives (A psychological thriller)

Evil In Disguise – a novel based on True events

Deadly Act (Hero series novella)

Torn Apart (Hero series #1)

End Result (Hero series #2)

In Plain Sight (Hero Series #3)

Double Jeopardy (Hero Series #4)

Criminal Actions (Hero Series #5)

Regrets Mean Nothing (Hero series #6)

Prowlers (Di Hero Series #7)

Sole Intention (Intention series #1)

Grave Intention (Intention series #2)

Devious Intention (Intention #3)

Cozy mysteries

Murder at the Wedding

Murder at the Hotel

Murder by the Sea

Death on the Coast

Death By Association

Merry Widow (A Lorne Simpkins short story)

It's A Dog's Life (A Lorne Simpkins short story)

A Time To Heal (A Sweet Romance)

A Time For Change (A Sweet Romance)

High Spirits

The Temptation series (Romantic Suspense/New Adult Novellas)

Past Temptation

Lost Temptation

Clever Deception (co-written by Linda S Prather)

Tragic Deception (co-written by Linda S Prather)

Sinful Deception (co-written by Linda S Prather)

PROLOGUE

"I won't be long, love, I'm just taking Mimi for a walk around the park," Amelia called up the stairs to her husband.

They generally took it in turns to walk their Bichon Frise bundle of fluff. She always felt guilty about leaving her at home all day long, not something she would have chosen to do, given the choice, but her husband, Eduardo, had surprised her with Mimi for her birthday back in the summer.

She sighed and removed her pampered pooch's lead and coat from the rack in the hallway. She bent to slip them on. "It's a bit fresh out there today. Blowing a fair gale, it is, little one, so we'd better wrap up warm."

She looked up to see Eduardo coming down the stairs with a huge grin on his constantly tanned face. Amelia stood upright and kissed him.

"Do you want me to come with you tonight?" he asked.

"No, I'd much rather you start preparing the evening meal. I'm starving, and one of your paellas would go down a treat, just saying."

He winked and swooped in for another cheeky kiss. "Ah, you love my paellas, don't you?"

"It brightens my day, gives me something to look forward to, to come home to Mimi and to tuck in to one of your delicious meals. I won't be long. The quicker I get going the sooner I'll be back. We could watch a film tonight, if you haven't got any extra work to do."

Her husband ran a food export company. They had moved from Liverpool around a year ago. To begin with, he'd had reservations about the move, but Amelia had worked her magic on him. It wasn't like they had any immediate family down south. Her parents had retired to the Lake District and, for years, had pleaded with her and Eduardo to join them. Once she and her husband had visited the village on the outskirts of Workington where her parents lived, that was it, she'd been smitten, had fallen hook, line and sinker and had put a deposit down that weekend on a rental cottage close to her parents.

"I haven't. I successfully cleared my desk before coming home," Eduardo said, his Spanish accent sending a thrill racing up her spine, as usual.

"Okay, I won't hang around then. This little one will be desperate for a wee. I'll be back shortly, within half an hour or so, darling."

"That'll give me enough time to work on my masterpiece."

She leaned in for another kiss, slipped on her dog-walking jacket and shoes, then set off. On the way to the park, she passed the usual regulars she normally said hello to at that time of evening. Mimi tugged on the lead, eager to get to her favourite park and play with her friends.

Amelia reflected on her day at work. She was a primary school teacher, and it had been a tough day. One of her colleagues had complained about her to the head and she'd been pulled over the coals. She'd objected and stamped her foot for ten minutes in her boss's office until she'd finally conceded it was probably a clash of personalities at play. There was a point during the confrontation that Amelia had considered jacking in her job. And if she and Eduardo hadn't been saving up to start a family, she would have quite happily done it without blinking an eye.

"That would have been perfect, being at home with you all day, sweetheart, wouldn't it?"

Mimi looked up at her and wagged her tail but pulled harder on the lead to get to the park.

Amelia laughed and upped her pace slightly. "All right, I'm going as fast as I can. I haven't got youth on my side, not like you, not these days."

They reached the entrance of the park, and Amelia surveyed the area to see if there were any—what she classed as—dangerous dogs close by. With the coast all clear, she let Mimi off her lead and threw the squidgy ball for her. They played fetch a few times until Mimi got fed up and wandered off to have a sniff around. Amelia took the opportunity to catch up on her messages on Facebook while she walked, oblivious to her surroundings.

"Nice evening." A woman walked past with a collie straining on its lead.

"Sorry." Amelia glanced up and smiled. "Work, you know how it is, never-ending, even out when enjoying a walk with the dog."

"Don't worry. We all lead busy lives these days, don't we? I saw your dog head over towards that small clump of trees."

Her cheeks heated up. "That'll teach me to pay attention. Thanks for the tip." She slotted her phone into her jacket pocket and sprinted down the path to the trees. "Mimi, where are you? Here, girl. What's Mummy got?" She kept her tone nice and light, in the hope that Mimi would come back quicker. She didn't, so Amelia ventured into the trees. It was very light still, just overcast and chilly for May. "Come here, you little rascal. Where are you? Mummy has some treats for you."

A squeal came from the trees and she sprinted into the wooded area.

"Mimi, are you hurt, baby? Come to Mummy."

A movement startled her up ahead. A man emerged from behind one of the older trees. Amelia gasped. He was holding Mimi. Not sure what to make of the situation, Amelia smiled and held out her arms.

"There you are, you little minx. Thank you so much for catching her. Once she takes off there's no keeping up with her."

The man's eyes narrowed. "Careless of you, to let her wander off alone like that, especially if you're preoccupied with that phone of yours."

"Excuse me? It was business. Besides, I don't have to explain myself to you. You can give me Mimi now. Thank you again, you can let her go now."

He squeezed Mimi's middle, and she squealed and wriggled in his arms, kicking up a fuss at being restrained.

"No, please, you're hurting her. She doesn't like to be held like that. If you'll just hand her over and we'll be on our way." Amelia took a few steps closer to the man. "Hush now, Mimi, everything is going to be all right."

"Is it?" the man sneered. "How can you be so sure?"

"What do you want from me? Please, let my dog go, you're hurting her."

With that, he dropped Mimi. She fell to the ground with a thud and ran off.

Amelia stared at the man, her insides bubbling with rage. She had to bite her tongue to prevent the angry verbiage from spilling out of her mouth. Had it emerged, it would have been full of expletives. Instead, she offered up a tight smile and said, "Thank you for letting her go."

He grinned, and as Amelia turned her back on him, he pounced on her, knocking her to the ground.

"What are you doing? Leave me alone. Get your hands off me. Let me go. My husband is in the park, he'll come looking for me. You won't get away with this."

He flipped Amelia over and slapped her around the face, first one side and then the other. "Shut the fuck up, you hear me? You're going to give me what I want, and then I'll set you free. Any shit from you, and I'll slit your throat, got that?"

Tears brimmed, and she nodded. His hands roamed her body. She squeezed her eyes shut, blocking out the pleasure and devilment taunting her in his gaze.

Please, God, don't let him do this to me. Not now, not ever. I just want to go home to Eduardo. I don't want this to happen.

The sound of the man's zip being opened forced her to look up at him. He was glaring at her, an evil expression casting a shadow over his features. His hands tore at her skirt, raising it above her knees. She tried to struggle, but his weight suppressed her attempt to move.

"Please, no, don't do this."

"Give me one good reason, and maybe I'll let you go."

She said the first thing that popped into her head. "Because I'm pregnant and you may harm my child."

He went still. His hands stopped for the slightest pause, only to begin their vile journey of violating her in the most intimate of places. He flicked her knickers aside and entered her. Amelia cried out. He slapped a hand over her mouth, quashing her objection. The ordeal took all of five minutes, although to Amelia it appeared to go on forever. Tears trailed down her cheeks; his hand was still clasped over her mouth after he'd completed his violent act.

Once she'd stopped struggling, he released his hand, but it

came with a warning, "It's not too late to kill you. Scream, and I'll carry out my threat."

"I won't, I promise." She shoved her skirt down and got to her feet.

The man stood only a couple of feet from her. Her stomach lurched, and she could feel the vomit rising and burning the back of her throat. She turned to empty her stomach, and he tutted behind her. A twig snapped, and then she felt something cold against her throat. She grasped her neck, and it was covered in liquid in no time at all. Blood. Her blood. She was in total shock as she tumbled to her knees, unable to cry out.

She stared up at him and mouthed, "Why?"

He laughed, leaned down to within a few inches of her face and whispered, "Because I can. I do a lot of things I'm not supposed to. I enjoy it. Causing panic in women. Violating them. Treating them like the weaker sex, because let's face it, that's what you are at the end of the day."

Amelia released the grip on her throat, lashed out at him, but he jumped back, and she fell flat on her face. Leaves rustled behind her, and she knew she was alone.

"Help me..." Her voice was low; there was no way she could cry out to gain a passerby's attention. "Mimi, help me. Come back, girl, and help me."

Leaves rustled behind her again, and she closed her eyes, pretending to be dead, dreading to think what the man would do to her next if he found her still alive. She didn't have it in her to try to move to see if it was him. A whimper sounded; it was Mimi.

"Mimi, go get help for Mummy, darling."

Mimi curled up in a ball beside her, and that was the last Amelia knew. They both fell asleep together after their terrifying ordeal.

CHAPTER 1

DI Sam Cobbs had finished work for the day and had rushed home to take the dogs out for a walk with Rhys. Little Casper had fitted in well to their family setup. He and Sonny played hard and snuggled up together during their downtime, like they had always been together. Rhys took Casper to work with him. Reports were mixed. Sometimes he was a bit of a handful in the therapist's office, but Rhys said that his antics had a pleasing effect on his clients. Casper succeeded in bringing them out of their shells and helped them to open up about their problems to Rhys.

Doreen still cared for Sonny during the day, which made the evenings interesting, to say the least. Here they were, on their evening stroll around the park, still conscious that they shouldn't allow Casper to walk too far, being only three months old, but once they got home it meant that Sonny and Casper curled up together in their large bed rather than tearing around the house all evening, disrupting Sam and Rhys's chill-out time together.

They wandered along the path, hand in hand, discussing the ups and downs of each other's day. It was during a slight pause in their conversation that Sam's ears pricked up and she caught the sound of a dog crying.

"Did you hear that?" She stopped and raised a finger to her lips. "Listen."

Rhys cocked an ear and pointed at the wooded area to the left of them. "It's coming from in there."

Without saying a word, Sam handed Sonny's lead to Rhys and took off.

"Hey, don't put yourself at risk. We should go in there together, Sam."

"I'm fine, I'll be right back. I have to find out what's going on, a dog might be hurt."

"Okay, we'll hang around here and wait for you. Give me a shout if you need a hand."

"I will." Sam ran into the woods and called out, "Hello, is anyone here?"

The dog yapped excitedly, but Sam had trouble pinpointing where the noise was coming from. She searched behind several of the shrubs littering the area and came away disappointed. Stopping, she faltered to find her bearings, and when the dog barked again, she took off in the only direction she was yet to try.

A small dog appeared in front of her on the woodland path and then disappeared again. She sprinted to the spot where she'd seen it and called out, then followed the dog's barking that was now close by on the right.

Her heart fluttered when she saw the woman's body. The dog was running up and down at the side of her. Sam approached and spoke to it gently; it was clearly terrified. "It's okay, sweetheart. Help is here now. I need to get to your mummy. Will you allow me to come closer?"

Sam inched forward, and the dog lunged, trying to bite her. She stood still and assessed the woman from the view she had of her, but Sam struggled to make out if the woman had just fainted or was seriously injured. Chancing her arm, she took another few steps closer, and that's when she spotted the blood coming from the woman's throat. Sam dipped a hand into her pocket to pull out her phone.

"Damn, I haven't got a reception. Shit!" She ran back to the clearing and tried again.

"Sam, what's wrong?" Rhys asked.

"A woman is either injured or dead back there. I can't get near her because the dog is protecting her, but I know she needs an ambulance."

"Leave it to me. I'll call them. You get back in there. Has the dog got a lead?"

"There's one lying next to the woman. I'll see if I can attach it and tie the dog to a nearby tree. Hurry, Rhys, it could be a matter of life or death."

"Go. I'll sort it."

Sam bolted back to the victim, and the dog again pounced, ready to sink its teeth into her ankle. She didn't care, all she knew was that she needed to get to the woman, and quickly. So what if the little terror latched on to her ankle bone? She picked up the lead, and when the dog struck again, she caught it by the collar, hooked the lead on and dragged it over to one of the slim tree trunks on the right.

"Is that you, Mimi?" she asked, finally recognising the dog.

Mimi's head tilted to the side, and she ceased barking. Sam patted her on the head and then went to check on the woman. She felt for any sign of life and found a faint pulse at the woman's neck. This excited her and yet struck the fear of God into her at the same time, having the woman's life in her hands.

The woman stirred for the briefest of moments and whispered, "Help me."

Sam got down close and smoothed the stray hairs from

her face. "Hang in there, help is on the way." She strained an ear to listen to the woman again but there was nothing except the sound of sirens in the distance. Sam gently shook the woman's shoulder. "Please, stay with me. Help is only a few minutes away now."

Mimi barked then whimpered and strained on her lead to get to her mummy.

"It's okay, sweetheart. Mummy can't give you cuddles right now. Soon, sweetie, soon."

The next few minutes were some of the most anxious Sam had ever encountered. She tried to get a response from the victim, but it was no good. Thankfully, the paramedics arrived and gently shoved Sam aside. She quickly ran through how she had discovered the woman. The older paramedic got down on his knees beside the victim and tried to strike up a conversation with her. However, as soon as he checked her vital signs, he glanced up at Sam and shook his head.

"No, you can't give up on her. She spoke to me. Pleaded with me to help her…"

"I'm sorry. She's lost a great deal of blood and…"

"Sam? Is everything all right?" Rhys tugged on her arm.

She didn't mean to but she shrugged his hand off.

"She's gone. I failed her. I let her down when I could have saved her." Sam crumpled to her knees and slapped her hands over her cheeks.

"Hey, now then. You can't go blaming yourself, lass," the paramedic insisted. "You did your best. Any idea how long she'd been lying here with that wound?"

Sam looked up at him and heaved out a sigh. "I don't know. All I know is that she needed my help and I did nothing. Correction, I let her life slip away."

"You're wrong to think that," the other male paramedic assured her. "You can see the state she's in. Even if we'd arrived half an hour ago, I doubt if we would have been able to save her. Give yourself a break. You did what you could with limited resources at your disposal."

"But five minutes ago, she was alive and talking to me."

"Talking? I doubt very much if she was capable of doing that, not with the size of that wound."

Sam nodded. "Okay, maybe talking was the wrong word to use. She whispered, at least she tried to communicate. The fact remains that I let her down. I neglected to save her."

"You can't blame yourself, Sam, I won't allow you to do that. It's the person who did this to her who is responsible for her losing her life, not you, you hear me?" Rhys said, his tone resolute with a note of caring attached.

The younger paramedic stepped closer to Sam and placed a hand on her arm. "Leave her to us. You've done your best for her."

Sam nodded and wiped away a lone tear rolling down her cheek. "You can't take her. This is a crime scene, and you're trampling all over it, all of you. Get back," she demanded, flipping into professional mode. "SOCO should do the necessary checks around here, and the pathologist needs to attend the scene."

"She's right," the older paramedic said. "We'll make a note on the log and touch base with control before we head off."

"Whatever," Sam replied. She peered over her shoulder at Rhys. "You'd better take the dogs home. I can't leave her here alone. I'll wait for the Forensic team to arrive."

"If you're sure," Rhys replied, seemingly dejected by her rejection. He turned and walked away with Casper and Sonny.

Sam's emotions were in turmoil, sadness the overwhelming sensation as she watched him go. That was until the younger paramedic nudged her with his elbow.

"Something tells me you're going to regret sending him off with a flea in his ear like that."

"I didn't. I'm a serving police officer and I've assigned myself to this case. How can I not when... I let the victim down?"

"Maybe you should dismiss yourself if you feel that way," the older paramedic suggested.

"Yep, I totally agree with Roy on that one. Pass the case on to someone else, for your own peace of mind, is it sergeant or inspector?"

"The latter. DI Sam Cobbs."

"Well, Inspector Cobbs, if I were in your shoes," the younger one said, "I would be passing it over before the rest of the mob descend on this place."

"It's not going to happen. I feel responsible and have no intention of running scared of this case. Now if you'll excuse me, gents, I need to check the victim over, see if I can find any form of identification for her." She reached into her pocket and extracted a pair of nitrile gloves and snapped them over her slender fingers.

Both men took a step back with their bags.

"We'll make the calls to the control centre from the vehicle and leave you to it."

"Thanks for all your help and the much-needed pep talk, guys."

"You're welcome. Take care of yourself and stop putting yourself under unnecessary pressure. This wasn't your fault, Inspector," the older paramedic said.

Sam smiled and followed them back through the woods to the clearing where she put in a call to Des, the pathologist. She closed her eyes, cringing when his abrupt tone rippled down the line. "Hi, It's Sam. I've got a new case for you."

"What? I was on my way home."

"A woman has lost her life tonight, she's had her throat

cut, and I'd rather not leave her body lying around out in the elements, if it's all the same to you."

"All right, there's no need to get your hand up your arse."

"I haven't. I'm simply stating facts."

"You'd better give me the location."

"It's Trinity Park, close to where I live."

"So you are at home, is that what you're saying?"

"I'll tell you all about it when you get here. I'll hang around until you arrive and then I'm going to have to shoot off to tell the next of kin."

"Ah yes, that undesirable task. I'll be there in less than fifteen minutes, the van is all set to go."

"Thanks, Des. See you soon. I'll get everything else organised."

"You do that. And don't let anyone trample over my crime scene."

"I'll do my best, although saying that, the paramedics had to attend to the victim because when I found her she was still alive."

"Shit, on all fronts. And you let her die?"

"Talk about sticking the knife in. Couldn't you have worded that better? I feel bad enough as it is."

"Sorry, I spoke without engaging my brain. Enough of this chatter, I'll be there shortly."

Sam ended the call and contacted the station to request backup. The area would need to be cordoned off at several points to prevent the general public from getting a closer look at the victim once the body had been processed. She finished her calls and headed back to fetch Mimi; the poor dog must be traumatised. With Mimi bouncing up and down beside her, Sam exited the wooded area and bumped into one of her dog-walking friends.

"Hello, Sam. Have you got a new dog? No, wait, isn't that Mimi?"

"Hi, Jenny. It is. I don't suppose you happen to know where she lives, do you?"

"Found her running around loose, have you?"

"Not exactly." Sam sighed and inhaled a steadying breath. "I'm afraid her owner has been involved in a serious crime. I need to get this little one home and speak to the family."

"Amelia or Eduardo?"

"Amelia," Sam confirmed. Mimi settled down beside her.

"Goodness. What type of crime, or can't you tell me?"

"I'd rather not say."

Jenny peered over her shoulder and jabbed a thumb at the ambulance. "I saw them arrive. I presumed it couldn't be much if they went back to their vehicle."

"Do you know where Amelia lives?" Sam asked, careful not to use the past tense.

"Three doors up from me. Twenty, Tennison Avenue."

"Thanks. Once the other teams arrive, I'll get Mimi back home to her dad."

"Umm... Amelia isn't... dead, is she?" Jenny asked, her mouth gaping open at her own question.

"I can't comment. I'm sorry, it's more than I dare do right now."

"Oh heck, I can see it on your face and in your eyes. She is dead, isn't she?"

Sam gulped and nodded. "Please, you can't say anything to anyone, not yet, not until I've broken the news to Eduardo."

"Oh my, this is just awful. Is she in there?" Jenny pointed behind Sam.

"Yes. I found Mimi in there, barking, trying to wake her mother. Sorry, that's all I can say for now. I shouldn't have told you that much. I'm so cut up about this. I came here for a quiet walk with my fella and our two dogs, never dreamt I would have to start work again at this time of night."

"How dreadful for you, Sam. Thank you for going the extra mile for a fellow dog walker. Eduardo will be broken when he hears the news. He loved her so much; they loved each other." She shuddered and waved. "I'm going to leave you to it. The evening has developed a chilly atmosphere."

"Take care of yourself, can you call someone from home to come and meet you? I need to ask you to keep this information to yourself for now."

"Don't worry. I'll ring my husband, I won't say anything, I wouldn't know where to start anyway."

She watched the distraught Jenny turn and walk away from her. Sam paced the area with Mimi agitated once more, by her side. "Come on, sweetie, everything will be all right. I'll take you home soon."

Over the next twenty minutes, several of the other dog walkers she regularly spoke to stopped to say hello and make a fuss of Mimi. Sam could see the inquisitiveness in their eyes, but she did her best to bat away or swerve any questions they had regarding the dog. She also warned them to go home as a crime had been committed and they might not be safe, thinking of her duty of care to the public. She let out a relieved sigh when she saw Des and his team coming through the park.

"Thank God you're here. I'm going to have to get this little one back home now."

"Go, you've given me enough to be going on with. Take the dog and run. Leave all of this to us. One thing before you go: how many people were close to the scene?"

"Four… two paramedics, me and my fella. Oh, and my two dogs plus this one here. I suppose you'll need to count them as well."

"Hardly. Thanks for the heads-up, though. Through here, is she?"

"I'll show you and then be on my way."

"That's decent of you," Des replied abruptly.

"I'm all heart, you should know that about me by now." Sam entered the wooded area and led Des and a couple of members of the Forensic Team to the clearing where Amelia's body was lying.

"Ouch, yep, she didn't stand a chance, not with her throat slit open like that."

"I know, it's horrendous, isn't it? I was shocked that she lasted long enough to speak to me."

"Did she give any indication of when the crime took place?"

"No, she said two words, 'help me', and then faded away."

"By that, it would indicate that the crime had not long taken place because there is no way she could have survived any length of time, not with that wound."

Sam shuddered involuntarily. "Don't say that. She could have been me."

"I doubt it, you said you were out here with your boyfriend." He clicked his finger and thumb together. "Now there's a thought. Maybe the boyfriend or her other half did it."

"Nope, I'm putting my neck on the line here and saying that you're way off the mark with that assumption."

Des raised an eyebrow and inclined his head. "How do you know?"

"I know her and her husband. Granted, only to say hello to down here at the park. They always seem happy enough, either holding hands or cuddling each other when they walk past me. If they had problems in their marriage, let's just say, they hid it well."

"Still worth checking out, not that I'm trying to tell you how to do your job."

"No, you'd never be guilty of doing that, would you?"

"Anyway, I have to get on. My wife is already livid at me

for cancelling our date night this evening. Her mother is babysitting the kids for us."

The leaves rustled behind them.

Sam followed Des's intense gaze.

"Kathryn, I told you to come right away, not hours later."

Des's assistant coloured up. Her gaze flicked between Des and Sam, and she stammered, "I'm sorry. I got lost. My satnav needs replacing and…"

Des silenced her with a raised hand. "I've heard enough of your excuses lately to last me a lifetime. Either you buck your ideas up, young lady, or maybe I should look at replacing you."

Sam tutted and snarled at Des, "This is neither the time nor place to have such a discussion, Professor Markham."

Des nodded. "You're right. I apologise," he mumbled, then added, "Kathryn, we'll talk about this in the morning. Go to the van and fetch me the two cases on the left. You've got your spare key, I take it?"

She dug in her pocket and held up a keychain with a single key dangling from it. "I have. I'll be back shortly."

"Sooner than that, if you value your job."

As soon as Kathryn left the area, Sam let him have it with both barrels. "Don't do that. You should never put members of your team down in front of other work colleagues or strangers."

"And you shouldn't go around dishing out unwanted advice until you're sure of the situation. She's on her final warning."

"What the fuck for?" Sam demanded through gritted teeth.

"Screwing up once too often. You have no idea what I have to put up with. She, and she only, makes my job ten times harder than it needs to be. She's supposed to assist me, you know, to ease my burden throughout the day. She doesn't, never has done. I have to check and double-check every piece of information she gives me, which in the end, slows down every case and gets people like you on my back."

"Are you sure? She's always seemed pretty eager to please you when I'm around."

"Oh yes, she's that all right, but standing around with your tongue hanging out like an overenthusiastic puppy has its limit, I'm sure you'll agree."

"Maybe you're being too harsh in your assumption there. She adores you. Mmm... maybe that's the wrong choice of word to use. Let me try again: she admires you and the work you do. Give her a break, man."

"I neither have the time nor the inclination to do such a thing, Inspector, not when I have impatient people like you breathing down my neck, wanting their PM results ASAP."

"Don't turn your foul mood on me. All I'm doing is chasing PMs so that I can get the evidence to throw at the sick individuals creating crime scenes such as this and robbing people of their lives. If that's wrong, then slap me down, but don't take it out on Kathryn."

"I don't. Stop talking out of your arse, Inspector. Didn't you say you had to be on your way?"

"I can take a hint. I'm going before I let rip. Be kind, Des, that's all I'm saying. Maybe Kathryn has got things going on at home that you're not aware of."

"I've got news for you, Sam, haven't we bloody all? You're a prime example, or you were when that waste-of-space husband of yours was still alive. Whilst at work you left all that angst and trauma behind you, didn't you? If you can do it, then so can others. Now that's all I have to say on the subject."

"That was a low blow, bringing Chris into the conversation, and you know it." Sam spun on her heel, growled and left the area.

She set off along the park with Mimi by her side. Several uniformed officers acknowledged her as they headed towards the scene to tape off the area. Moments later, Kathryn came through the gates.

Sam stopped to speak with her. "Are you all right, Kathryn?"

"I will be, once this job is over, whenever that's likely to be."

"You shouldn't let him bully you like that."

"He's my boss. I've been slipping up now and again, he has a right to be narked with me."

Sam reached into her pocket and pulled out one of her business cards. "If you ever need to chat about anything, give me a shout."

"You're too kind. Please, I'll be fine. In fact, I have a job interview tomorrow."

"What? You're leaving?"

Kathryn hitched up her shoulders and dropped them again. "I think it's for the best. All I do, day in and day out, is piss him off. I don't think either of us is happy in our work at present."

"I'm sorry, I didn't realise things had got so bad between you. What job are you going for?"

Kathryn's gaze dropped to the ground, and she shuffled her feet. "It's at a restaurant, my friend works there. It's a busy place, and the tips are good. She gets a vast amount of job satisfaction from her work."

"Oh, okay. But does she have the qualifications you have under your belt?"

"No, but job satisfaction and being happy in your working life means a lot to me. I'll give it a go, if I get the job, see how I feel after a month or so, and if necessary, seek out a new adventure."

Sam cast a glance over her shoulder at the crime scene.

"My take is that if you hand in your notice, Des will be gutted. Yes, do it, it'll serve the old grouch right. He needs to learn how to respect his fellow colleagues and restrain himself."

"Thanks for caring, Inspector, it means a lot to me."

"Always. Ring me if you ever need to chat, got that? Whether you remain in the job or move on to pastures new."

"Thanks, I will. Enjoy the rest of your evening. Oops, I doubt if that will happen, will it?"

Sam smiled at the younger woman. "Hardly, I'm on my way to break the news to the victim's husband."

"I don't envy your job. That must be hard to take."

"I admit, I detest this side of the job but I'd rather do it and know it's been done right than have a colleague mess it up."

"I can understand that. Sorry, I'd better go, get the professor's equipment to him before he throws another hissy fit."

"Blame me if he kicks off. Good luck tomorrow, if that's the job you really want, Kathryn."

"It's not, however, it's clear to me and to Professor Markham that I'm not cut out for this role."

"I wish you'd reconsider. Over the years, too many women in your position have downed tools and run for the hills instead of standing their ground against the bullies."

"I no longer have any fight left in me. I'm sorry if you think I'm letting the side down."

Sam smiled. "I totally get that, and you're not letting anyone down, not if that's the way you feel. Life's too short to spend your working day doing something that is getting you down all the time. He's going to miss you when you go, you mark my words."

"I doubt it. Goodbye, Inspector. Maybe our paths will cross in the future. Not that I've got the job yet. If that falls through then I'll have to remain in my role until something else comes along."

"PMA."

"What's that?"

"Positive Mental Attitude—everyone needs it in their life."

"Ah, yes. I remember one of my teachers going on about it in my last year at school."

"There you go, you should always listen to what your teachers tell you. See you around, Kathryn."

They shared a smile and went off in their different directions. Sam walked up the road, took the right at the top, and then the first left. Number twenty was right in front of her as she turned the corner. Mimi whimpered beside her.

"Come on, sweetheart, let's go find Daddy to break the news."

They set off towards the small mid-terraced Victorian house that was situated in the middle of the row. The front door was on the pavement, not a garden in sight on either side of the road. She rang the bell, and the door was opened within seconds by Eduardo.

"Did you forget your ke…? Oops, sorry, I thought you were my wife. She's always forgetting her key."

Sam produced her warrant card. "Hello, Eduardo. I'm DI Sam Cobbs, can I come in and speak with you?"

It was then that he noticed Mimi at Sam's feet. "Mimi? What's going on?" He glanced up and down the road. "Where's Amelia? What's all this about? Where's my wife?" His voice rose two octaves, and he bent down to gather Mimi in his arms.

"Inside would be better, sir," Sam insisted.

He seemed disorientated but dipped back behind the door and motioned for her to enter.

Sam closed the door behind her and followed him

through the house to the kitchen at the rear where he lowered Mimi to the floor by her food bowl.

"Would it be all right if I take a seat?" Sam asked.

"Yes, excuse my manners. Go ahead. Please, tell me, where is my wife? And why do you have my dog?"

"I'm sorry to have to be the bearer of bad news, but whilst I was at the park earlier, I heard Mimi barking in the woodland area down there. When I went to investigate, she was standing next to Amelia."

He frowned and shook his head. "I don't understand. Please forgive me, sometimes my English isn't so good."

"You're doing really well. This is so very hard for me to tell you. This evening, a woman who we believe is your wife lost her life in a brutal attack."

He stood quickly, and the force tipped his chair backwards. Mimi yelped and ran out of the room. "Shit! She what? She's dead, is that what you're telling me?"

Sam nodded. "I'm so sorry, Eduardo."

"I can't believe what I'm hearing. Amelia... she went to the park to walk the dog, and someone... someone killed her? Why? Have you caught them?"

"No, when I arrived at the scene there was no one else around."

He righted his chair again and sat heavily. He placed his elbows on the table, his hands covering his face then his head. "No, no, no, I can't believe what you're telling me. My beautiful Amelia, she is gone. Never going to come home again. But why?" His hands dropped to the table, and his gaze latched on to Sam's.

"I don't have the answers for you, I wish I did."

He raised a pointed finger at Sam. "I know you, don't I?"

"Yes, I walk my dogs at the park with my partner. I think Mimi recognised me, that's why she came home willingly with me."

"Mimi. Mimi, here, girl," he called out, his voice breaking on a sob. The terrified dog appeared in the doorway and hesitated for a second or two until Eduardo reached behind him on the shelf and grabbed the treat jar to entice the ball of fluff. "Come on, sugar. It's just you and me now, baby." He sniffled and wiped his nose on the back of his hand, mumbled an apology and got to his feet to tear off a sheet of kitchen towel. "How can I take this in? I can't believe this news. We were... only last night... talking about having a baby, and now all our hopes and dreams have gone, along with her. How will I cope without her?"

"I'm sorry, I can't imagine how you must be feeling at this time, and if I offer words of condolence, you might think that I'm delivering them without genuine concern for you. Just know that you're not alone. I can assign a family liaison officer to be with you, if you want one."

"Is that what people do at times like this? Accept the help of strangers? Invite a stranger to sit with them while they grieve the loss of a loved one?"

"Some people find it a great source of comfort. The choice is yours and yours alone. Everyone deals with grief differently. Nothing is set in stone in dire circumstances such as this."

"I want to break down but I'm too much of a man to do it in front of a woman, it's not what my father taught me to do as a child. But my heart is shattered into a thousand tiny pieces. Why did this happen to my beautiful wife? She left the house less than an hour ago to take Mimi for her usual walk and... never came back home. How is that right?"

Sam sighed, her heart lying heavy in her chest as the waves of sorrow flowed from the man. "I don't have the answers for you, not at this time, but I want to assure you that I won't stop seeking the truth, not if it takes the final breath from my body. I don't want to go into details about how your wife died, it's not my place to do that. What I will tell you is that no one, male or female, should have been subjected to what she went through at the end of her life."

His hands covered his head, and he shook it. "I can't listen to this. Please, don't tell me any more. I want to remember her as she was." He glanced sideways at the wedding photo hanging on the wall next to him. "She was perfect, in each and every way. I had girlfriends before she came along, but no one has ever come close to her. My love for her grew more every single day I woke up next to her. I would sit up in the morning, watching her sleep peacefully beside me. Never again will I feel the power of our love."

His heartfelt speech was interrupted by the front door opening and a woman's voice calling out, "Amelia, Eduardo, I'm here."

His eyes widened, and he shot out of his chair. Mimi barked, and an older woman appeared in the doorway.

"Oh, I see you have a visitor. Forgive my intrusion, is Amelia upstairs?" she asked.

"Oh, hello, Cathy. Umm… I think you need to come in and take a seat."

The woman entered the room warily, her gaze shifting quickly between Eduardo and Sam. "Is something going on here?"

"It's not what you think," Eduardo assured her.

He pulled out the chair next to his, and she sat and stared at Sam.

"Then what is it, and who are you?" she demanded.

Sam smiled tightly. "Hello, Cathy. I'm DI Sam Cobbs of the Cumbria Constabulary."

"You're from the police?" A hand slapped against her cheek and trembled. "Why do I get the feeling I'm not going to like what I'm about to hear?"

Eduardo moved his chair slightly closer to Cathy's and gathered her free hand in his. "Cathy, you need to be strong."

She tried to wrench it out of his grasp, all the time shaking her head as tears bulged and threatened to fall. Eduardo refused to let her go.

"Is she dead?" Cathy whispered eventually.

Eduardo nodded and reached out his arms to her. She twisted in her seat to face him and slipped into them.

Sam would have had to have a heart made of stone not to be affected by the pure outpouring of grief from the two people whose worlds she had come here tonight to shatter. "I'm so very sorry for your loss."

It took a while for the tears to subside and for Cathy to release her hold on Eduardo. She pulled back and stared at Sam. "When? Where? How?"

"Earlier this evening, at the park while she was out with Mimi. I can't share the details with you, not yet. I left the pathologist and a Forensic Team at the scene."

"Oh God, that means it's bad, doesn't it? Did someone kill her intentionally? Is that what you're hinting at?"

Sam swallowed down the acid that had seeped into her throat and nodded. "Yes. I'm sorry. I came here as quickly as I could to share the news with Eduardo."

"Mimi. How did she get home? By herself?" Cathy asked, confused.

"No. I brought her home. I know Amelia and Eduardo from walking my dogs in the same park. I didn't know where they lived, but another of our mutual friends at the park filled in the details for me and I came straight here. I felt it was my duty to be the one to tell Eduardo."

"I suppose we should be grateful to have someone as caring as you on the case. Will you be in charge of the investigation?" Cathy asked.

"I will make sure I am."

"Do you know why it happened?"

"No, not yet. Amelia was alive when I found her but slipped away. I did my best to try to save her, but the paramedics assured me that there would have been nothing I could have done, given the extent of her injuries."

"So she suffered before she left us?" Cathy choked out the words.

"I'm sorry, there's no easy way to tell you this, but yes."

"Why? Why my baby?" Cathy sobbed.

"I know this is a difficult time for you both, but if there is anything you think I should know, it'll help me to get the investigation off the ground."

Cathy shook her head. "Like what? She was a primary school teacher. Who could she have upset enough for someone to set out to kill her?"

Sam removed the notebook she always carried in her pocket and flipped it open. "Which school?"

"The one in the village, it's the only one here. I still can't believe that someone would want to kill my baby. Murder her, why?"

"I have to ask if there have been any awkward incidents in recent weeks. If Amelia has had any reason to fall out with anyone, that sort of thing."

Eduardo and Cathy stared at each other for a long time.

"I can't think of anything, no," Eduardo was the first to confirm.

"I agree. She would have told us," Cathy said. "Or would she? What if someone was making her life hell and she kept that from us at the end? We're never going to find the person who did this to her, are we? If you don't have anything to go on, how can you ever convict someone for the crime they've committed? For robbing us of our dear, sweet Amelia?"

"Don't worry, it's surprising where leads come from. The investigation hasn't begun yet. I promise you this, I won't rest until I've caught the person responsible. You have my word."

"But how can you say that when you have nothing to go on? Am I being thick here?" Cathy asked.

Eduardo gripped her hands tighter. "Let's leave the inspector to figure out how she's going to do it. Did Amelia have any secrets from me?" he asked, a pained expression distorting his handsome features.

Cathy looked him in the eye and said one word. "No. She loved you, Eduardo, you were her life. She would never have kept such a thing from you. What would she have gained from that?"

"It's as I thought. Forgive me, Cathy, I'm so confused right now, I had to ask."

"There's no need for you to apologise. Don't ever doubt the love she had for you, not now, today, next week, or ever come to that. She loved you with every beat of her heart and more."

"I know. I don't think I will ever feel the same again, now that she is no longer with us."

"It's just not something you hear about in a small village like ours, is it?" Cathy asked.

"Had this happened a few years ago, I would have agreed with you," Sam said.

Cathy narrowed her eyes. "What you're saying is that the crime rates in this area are out of hand and the police are out of their depth? Go on, admit it."

"Cathy, you can't say that. The inspector is going to help us, she said so," Eduardo stepped in to defend Sam.

"I'm certainly going to try, Eduardo. I'm sorry you feel that way, Cathy. You're right, crime rates have escalated to an all-time high since before the pandemic, and we're often overwhelmed as a force, but what I can tell you is that my team is fully committed to the cause, no matter what life throws at us. I also want to assure you that we have a very high success rate."

"I'm glad you're on our side," Eduardo said with a sigh. "And you should be, too, Cathy."

"I am. I'm sorry. My emotions are in turmoil. I'm struggling to deal with them and just lashing out."

Sam raised a hand. "It's to be expected, there's no need for you to apologise. What about ex-partners, did Amelia have any?"

Cathy's mouth turned down at the sides. "I don't want this to come out the wrong way, but yes, she's had a few over the years. You know how beautiful she was."

"I do. A very pretty lady. Anything there, do you think? That I should perhaps look into?"

"I can't think of anything right now. Can I get back to you later? What about you, Eduardo? Has Amelia mentioned any of her exes being in touch and causing problems lately?"

"No, nothing. All was good for both of us. We had a very happy life, not that we would let anyone in to disrupt it. Well... that's what we thought. Now this has happened, I find myself questioning so many things. There is no reason why someone should kill her, ruin our happy lives like this."

"I agree with him," Cathy said. "What gives someone the right to do it? To force such changes in an otherwise stable and happy relationship?"

Sam shrugged. "I'm not saying someone has specifically targeted Amelia. This might have been a random attack at the park, but it would be wrong of me not to ask."

"We understand," Cathy replied. "What now? Can we see her?"

"I will pass on your details to the pathologist. He'll have to perform a post-mortem. That will take place over the next few days, and then he'll make contact with you, let you know when you can pay your last respects."

Eduardo gasped and shook his head. "Do we have to? I'm not sure I can put myself through such an ordeal."

Cathy smiled and threw an arm around his shoulder. "We'll do it together. She'd want us to be there, no matter how difficult it will be for us, Eduardo. We can't let her down now."

He sighed, and a fresh glut of tears dripped onto his cheeks. "I want to remember her the way she was. My beautiful angel. A part of me has died along with her tonight."

"I agree," Cathy said. "Neither of us will ever be the same."

Sam's heart lurched. Suddenly, guilt overwhelmed her, because when Chris had committed suicide a few months earlier, she had felt nothing but relief. But then, her love for him had died long before he'd taken his own life that night. "If there's nothing else, I think I should be going. I'll leave you a card each. Please don't hesitate to ring me, day or night, if you have any questions or if you think of anything that might help with the investigation."

Cathy picked up one of the cards and asked, "Will you begin this evening?"

"No, I'll make some notes when I get home, to get a head start on the investigation, however, the real work will begin in the morning, once my team has been assembled and made aware of the crime."

"In the meantime, there's a killer out there on the loose. How is that right?"

"Don't worry, there will be patrol cars circulating the area throughout the rest of the evening and into the night. If the killer is lingering, as some of them are inclined to do, anyone acting suspiciously will be picked up and taken to the station for questioning."

"I doubt if they would be foolish enough to hang around," Cathy said.

"Honestly, you'd be surprised." Sam rose from her seat.

She made a quick fuss of Mimi and then walked towards the kitchen door. "Please get in touch if you need me. I'll try and update you periodically during the investigation. I want to assure you that you have the right team working on the case."

"Don't let us down, Inspector," Cathy warned. "As a family, we deserve answers."

"I appreciate that, I sincerely do, and I can promise you I'll give this investigation one hundred percent."

Eduardo saw Sam to the front door. He peered over his shoulder and whispered, "I believe you. I think Cathy might take a bit of convincing."

"It's natural for her to be wary. I won't let you down. Again, Eduardo, I'm so very sorry for your loss."

"It's okay. You've been very kind and compassionate towards us this evening, I'm grateful for that."

Sam touched his arm gently. "Take care, Eduardo. I'll be in touch soon."

"Thank you. I hope you live up to your promise and find this vile person before very long."

Sam smiled. "That's the plan." She left the house and walked back home, using the next ten minutes to reflect on how short life could be for some folk.

Rhys came to greet her, along with the dogs, the minute she set foot through the front door. He gathered her in his arms, and the tears she'd been holding back all evening flowed freely. Sonny nuzzled her leg, and she dropped a hand to ruffle the soft hair on his head.

"I'm okay, honestly. I just needed to let go of all the pent-up emotions I've been carrying around with me since I found her."

"Come in, let me fix you a drink. I take it you'll be wanting something stronger than coffee."

"A glass of brandy would go down a treat right now."

"Leave it to me. Come on, boys, give your mum some space to move."

The three of them trotted off down the hallway into the newly renovated kitchen that she was still paying off, thanks to her ex, Chris, taking out a loan in her name without her knowledge of it. Sam removed her shoes and coat and took a moment to breathe before she ventured into the kitchen. She hoped Rhys didn't bombard her with questions that she didn't have the answers to over dinner. Not that she was in the least bit hungry.

"There you are," he said. "Take a seat. Are you up for eating? I've cooked salmon and made a salad with it."

"Sounds good to me. I'll try and manage some of it, if my stomach will allow it. I think it's still tied up in knots."

"Understandable. I caught a glimpse of the victim's wound." Rhys shuddered. "Who could do such a horrible thing to that beautiful young woman?" He raised a hand. "No, you don't want me going on about it, do you? Take a sip of your drink and try to relax."

"Thanks. I'd rather not discuss it this evening, if it's okay with you. I'll have to make some notes after dinner, not that I'm likely to forget what I saw this evening, but it's best to jot things down all the same. It's been a long day, and I'd hate to miss something important."

"Take all the time you need. I'll keep the boys occupied for a while."

"Thanks. How was Casper today?"

"Trying at times, but he's getting there. Once a client arrives and they've made a fuss of him, he goes back to his bed and falls asleep. Not bad, considering how young he is."

"I think he's going to be a smart dog just like his predecessor… and his father," she added quickly.

Rhys grinned. "Why thank you. Feeling a bit better now, are you?"

"A bit. The drink is definitely doing the trick. Can I help with dinner?"

"All done, just waiting on the salmon to finish cooking. The dogs have been fed and watered. I'll take them in the garden and wear them out after dinner, give you some peace and quiet to do your paperwork."

"Thank you, what would I do without you?"

He smiled, and her heart skipped several beats. It had been given a real workout over the last few hours, that was for sure. Sam nipped into the office to retrieve an A4 pad and took it back to the kitchen where she scribbled down some notes.

Once Rhys had served up the dinner, she set the pad aside. "This smells delicious. Thank you for looking after me so well."

He laughed. "It works both ways, you do your fair share other days. Dare I ask about the next of kin? I know they have to be the first to be informed."

"I've done it already. That's where I've been most of the evening. I left the pathologist and his team at the scene and went to see Amelia's husband. Her mother turned up a few minutes later, so I had to break the news to her as well."

"I don't envy you, love. That must be one of the toughest parts of the job for you."

"It is. But being unable to help a victim in need is also galling. That will remain with me for a long time." Sam tucked into her dinner but found it difficult to swallow anything past the lump lodged in her throat. She slid the plate to one side and apologised. "I'm sorry, it's refusing to go down."

"There's no need. Saying that, you need to eat to keep your strength up for the battle that lies ahead of you."

"You're a wise man, Rhys, but it won't go down. I'll try again later. I can always heat it up in the microwave."

He raised an eyebrow. "I think the salad ingredients might make a few objections to that notion."

Sam laughed. "What was I thinking? Ignore me, my head is elsewhere this evening."

"Why don't you take your drink into the lounge and finish off making your notes? I'll eat this and clear up the kitchen, then go out back and play with the dogs for a while."

"You're amazing, thank you. It shouldn't take me too long." She picked up her pen and notebook and retired to the lounge. Neither of the dogs joined her, they remained with Rhys, no doubt hoping for any scraps to be likely dropped by their dad.

First on the agenda was to place a call to the station. She spoke to the night shift desk sergeant. "Hi, it's DI Sam Cobbs. I attended the murder scene that took place in Trinity Park this evening."

"Ah, yes, ma'am, nasty incident by all accounts. What can I do for you?"

"I thought I'd touch base with you. Sorry I didn't call you earlier, I was busy, breaking the news to the next of kin."

"Ouch, no need to apologise, ma'am, you did the right thing, but you know that already."

"I do. I wanted to make sure you had several patrols in the area this evening, in case the killer is still out there, lingering, watching the shit show."

"It has been known in the past, you're right. And yes, I have a couple of cars patrolling the area. They've not discovered anything yet, but they're out there, keeping an eye on proceedings."

"Thanks. I knew you would have it all in hand. I'll bid you goodnight in that case."

"Try and enjoy the rest of your evening, ma'am."

"*Try* being the operative word, eh? Ring me if there are any developments to the case. Goodnight, Sergeant."

"Don't worry, I will."

Sam hung up and immediately got to work on her notes. The words flowed nonstop for the next twenty minutes. She set her notebook aside, stretched her arms out and yawned, then went back into the kitchen to find the boys. The room was empty, so she peered out of the window and saw the three of them playing fetch in the back garden.

She ventured out to see them. "Hey, I thought you'd all run off and deserted me."

Sonny and Casper came bounding towards her. Sonny sat at her feet, but the pup's momentum carried him into her aching calves.

"Casper!" Rhys shouted.

Sam steadied herself and held up a hand. "He's fine. He got a touch overexcited, that's all. Can I join in, or are you enjoying yourselves too much as a threesome?"

"Of course you can, although I think Casper's enthusiasm is waning a little. Come on, boys, fetch."

Sonny left Sam's side and bounced across the lawn to fetch the ball while Casper flopped to the ground and rested his tired head on his front paws.

Sam laughed. "I think you're right, someone has had enough, and it's not Sonny. I'll take him in, give you guys a break for a while."

"We won't be long. Sonny could do with a bit more exercise after his walk was cut short earlier."

"I feel bad about that. Sorry."

"Don't be, that's not why I mentioned it. Do me a favour and put the kettle on, will you?"

"Of course. Tea or coffee?"

"A coffee would be wonderful. See you in five."

Sam scooped the lethargic pup into her arms and nuzzled into his belly. "Come on, trouble, let's get you tucked up in bed. It won't be long before you're zonked out for the night."

Casper licked her face and tapped her nose with his paw. "You're going to be a little rascal and blight our lives for a few months yet, but I wouldn't have it any other way."

They went back into the house. She put Casper down by his water bowl, and he had a drink before his legs gave way beneath him again. Sam picked him up and put him on his bed in the corner. His eyes drooped instantly, and he was asleep within seconds.

She smiled and stared at him. "One tired pup. Your father's job is done for the day." She filled the kettle and prepared the cups with coffee granules, milk and sugar. "What I wouldn't give for a proper coffee right now."

"We could always get an espresso machine," Rhys said, coming inside with Sonny. "I have to agree, you do find yourself getting accustomed to the taste."

"We'll see how funds are at the end of the month, how's that? We could go halves."

Rhys took a step towards her and held his arms out. "Whatever is best for you. I don't mind buying one, though, it would be my contribution to the home we're now sharing."

"I know, and I love you for caring, but you've also got to realise that I'm an independent bugger at the best of times."

He laughed. "If that hasn't been obvious by now then I need to go back and do some extra training."

Sam kissed him. "You are funny. Halves or nothing, okay?"

"Whichever way you want to play it is fine by me. How did you get on with your notes?"

"All finished, so I can devote the rest of the evening to you and Sonny. I think Casper is out for the count."

"Maybe I let him run around too much. His poor wee legs need to develop properly and get much stronger."

"You haven't been out there for that long. He'll tell you when he's had enough. He loves playing with you and

Sonny." The kettle turned off, and she poured the boiled water into the mugs.

"Fancy a biscuit?"

"Why not? There's some shortbread in the tin."

The three of them transferred to the lounge and switched off the light but left the door open in case Casper woke up and fretted, wondering where they were.

It wasn't long before Sam's eyelids drooped. "I think I'll go up soon, if that's okay with you?"

"You don't have to ask my permission. You've had an exhausting day on top of what you've had to deal with this evening. How are you now, emotionally?"

She ran a finger around the rim of her mug. "Maybe you should ask me that question tomorrow. No, seriously, I think I'm all right. Or should I say, I'm better than I was earlier. Hopefully, the image of finding her and her trying to speak won't haunt me for the rest of the night."

"I'm here if you need to chat."

"Thank you, I know you are. I'm going to head upstairs."

"You go, I'll see to the dogs and be up soon."

He took her mug from her, and she leaned in for another kiss. They parted, and she whispered, "I love you, Rhys. Thank you for being kind and considerate of my needs."

"Nonsense. There are going to be days when I'm as exhausted as you are. I'll be expecting the tables to be turned when that day comes around."

"Don't worry, this is a partnership in every way. I'll be there for you, as and when you need me."

Sam left the room and made her way upstairs. She visited the bathroom, jumped in the shower to rid herself of any lingering smell of death on her body, not that there was any, and after drying her hair she slipped into bed. She made a conscious effort to block out Amelia's crime and was asleep within a few minutes. Rhys joined her a while later, and she stirred and snuggled up to him. They fell asleep in each other's arms, but a nightmare made her sit bolt upright at two-fifteen.

Rhys turned on the light beside him and asked, "Are you all right?"

"I'm okay, I think. I just need to block out that image. I thought I had conquered it, but the trouble is, my mind has other ideas."

He inched closer and gathered her in his arms. "Try to switch off."

"Believe me, I've tried."

He kissed her forehead and whispered, "Try harder."

He switched off the light and was asleep, gently snoring beside her, within seconds. In the end, Sam lay awake until four. She thought about getting up and going downstairs but held tight, determined not to disturb Rhys again. His job was just as demanding as hers.

Rhys woke her at seven with a cup of coffee and a slice of toast. "How did you sleep?"

"I dropped off at around four. I didn't wake after that, so not too bad. Are the dogs in the garden?"

"Yep, I've cleared up the puddle Casper deposited in the kitchen overnight."

"Bless him."

She drank her coffee and ate her toast and then started her day in earnest.

CHAPTER 2

$\mathcal{S}$am arrived at the station early and, ignoring the usual post awaiting her attention in her office, set about filling in the whiteboard with the new case. On the way in, she had checked with the desk sergeant to see if there had been any kind of developments overnight and was disappointed to learn there hadn't been any.

The investigation would begin as soon as her team was assembled. Bob Jones, her partner, was the first to arrive.

"Blimey, and there was me thinking I would be the first one here this morning. Everything all right?" He stood beside her and read the information on the board. "When did this happen?"

"Last night, when I got home. It occurred at the park where I take the dogs."

"And you found the victim?"

Sam gulped and nodded, the emotions swelling within her once more. "Yep. She was still alive when I found her. I did my very best to try and save her, but she drifted away."

"I'm not surprised if she had an extra smile in her throat."

Sam swiped his arm. "It's not funny. The inability to save a life is debilitating, mate, I assure you."

"Sorry, I didn't mean to make light of the situation. It must have been awful for you to deal with. Have you slept?"

"On and off during the night. I ended up being too scared to close my eyes."

"I thought as much. I think it would have affected me in the same way. You're going to need to get past the raw emotions, Sam, if we're going to catch the culprit."

"I know what I have to do, however, it's whether my mind is going to be able to switch off or not."

The door opened, and the rest of the team filtered into the room.

"Morning, guys. Get yourselves a coffee, and we'll get started on the new case."

The team fixed their drinks, murmuring about what they had already read on the board. Moments later, everyone had assembled in a semi-circle in front of Sam. She described the crime scene and what she had encountered in the hours after she'd arrived home the previous evening.

"It was horrendous, not something I'd wish on my worst enemy, I can tell you. Being rendered helpless like that."

"Hey, this had nothing to do with you, boss," Bob assured her. "With a gaping wound like that, if you think logically about it, there's no way she was going to survive."

"I agree with Bob," Claire was quick to add. "You couldn't have done anything else for her but be with her when she passed away. I bet that was a great source of comfort to her when the time came, boss."

Sam smiled at the sergeant. "No matter how many times I tell myself that, my heart and my head just aren't keen on communicating with each other at the moment."

"You're going to have to give it some time," Bob told her.

"I know. Anyway, I've checked with the desk sergeant this

morning. There were patrol cars in the park area last night, but nothing out of the ordinary has been reported. Before we even get cracking on this case, I need to make you aware that I believe our backs are going to be against the wall from the outset. We're talking about a small community here, there's no CCTV cameras to help us out. What we need to do is go back to basic policing on this one. I'm going to send four of you out there to canvass the area, see if anyone saw any possible strangers hanging around, either last night or sometime in the last week or so. The killer must have known the area. What we need to find out is whether he's a regular to the park or if he's visited the area and carried out surveillance before striking, assuming it's a man."

"It ain't going to be easy," Bob muttered.

"Didn't I just say that?" Sam snapped, her patience already tighter than a coiled spring.

"Sorry, I was just saying."

"No, you were stating the obvious, which we can all do without hearing. After the pathologist and his team arrived at the scene, I tracked down Amelia's address and went to break the news to her husband. Her mother showed up during the conversation. It was distressing, as you can imagine, but they spent some time with me, answering any questions I needed to ask. Their response to the most obvious question, if Amelia had fallen out with anyone in the past month or so, was a categorical no. She was a primary school teacher. Bob and I will drop over there first thing, see if they can give us any information."

"I suppose that's likely. What about the husband?" Bob asked.

"He's a lovely man. I didn't get any bad feelings as far as he's concerned. He seemed a very genuine person and even told me that he and Amelia were planning on starting a family soon."

"Aww… that's such a shame," Claire said. "What about the mother? Any ex-boyfriends that we should be delving into?"

"No, Amelia had plenty, but no one that either of them was willing to throw into the spotlight. So, I suggest that Liam, Suzanna, Oliver and you, Alex, head out there and start knocking on all the doors around the entrance to the park and in the roads surrounding it." Sam tutted. "I need to postpone going out to the primary school and concentrate on getting the word out there about the crime via a conference. Suzanna, why don't you and Liam visit the school instead? Have a word with the head and any teachers she's willing to make available, see if there's been anyone hanging around the school or if Amelia had confided in any of her colleagues about something that had been bothering her. To me, I think it's a long shot. I'm getting the feeling that Amelia was possibly in the wrong place at the wrong time."

"But we still need to do the extra digging in case," Bob said.

"Exactly."

"Want me to check into the financial status of the couple, boss?" Claire asked.

Sam nodded. "If you would, Claire. Let's see if there's anything there to be concerned about. Right, is everyone clear on their role today? Any further questions? No, right, let's get cracking, team, don't let me down."

The group tidied away their chairs, and the four members tasked with canvassing the area around the park and going to the school headed off.

"I'll be in my office, arranging the conference and going through my post." Sam carried what was left of her drink into the office. She peered out of the window at the dreary morning and sipped her drink while she watched the team jump into their cars and drive out of the station's car park. "Good luck, guys. You're going to need it, we all are."

"Talking to yourself again?"

Recognising the voice, Sam almost spilt her drink as she spun around to face DCI Alan Armstrong. "Sorry, sir. I didn't see you there."

He laughed and sat in the chair in front of her desk. "Unless you have eyes in the back of your head, I wouldn't expect you to, Inspector. Take a seat, I need a chat with you."

"Dare I say it? This sounds ominous. If it's about the paperwork from the last case I solved not being on your desk by now as promised…"

"It's not. Sit!"

Sam rushed to her seat and sat there staring gormlessly at her senior officer, waiting to be torn off a strip or two.

"You needn't look so worried. You've done nothing wrong, not that I'm aware of anyway. I caught wind of something being discussed in the reception area on my way in this morning and thought I'd check it out with you."

Sam's brow wrinkled into a confused frown. "You did?"

"A crime scene that occurred in a park last night. Maybe I'm wrong thinking that it would be one of your cases. I could have sworn I heard your name mentioned."

"Ah, yes, you heard right. I was the one who stumbled across the victim whilst I was out walking my dogs last night, sir."

"Dogs? I thought you only had the one. Never mind, carry on."

"My partner has a dog as well."

He nodded his understanding and gestured with his hand for her to fill him in. "You stumbled across the victim? Was she already dead?"

"No. She pleaded with me for help. I ran back to the clearing and called an ambulance, but it was too late. She died a few moments later."

"From what sort of injuries?"

"Her throat was cut." A shiver ran the length of her spine, and the image she'd successfully managed to suppress all morning came flooding back to haunt her.

"Are you okay?"

"I'm getting there. It's a tough one to deal with, letting someone's life slip through your hands."

He vehemently shook his head. "You mustn't think that. I have no doubt you did your best for her. You called the ambulance. I'm not sure I would have been able to do anything else had I been there."

"Thanks, I'm trying to think of it that way, but the raw emotion keeps throttling me when I least expect it."

"What are you saying? You want me to reassign the investigation to another team?"

"Oh no. I'd rather handle it myself, sir. I'm not doubting my capabilities, it's just going to take its toll on me emotionally."

He inclined his head. "Do you need to see the counsellor to help you process it?"

"No, I'll be fine. My partner is there if I need him."

"Am I missing something?"

"He's a psychiatrist." Try as she might to prevent the colour rising in her cheeks, she failed. "Sorry, I thought you knew."

"No, I'd heard rumours that you were shacked up with someone new."

Sam chuckled. "You make it sound so sordid. I thought we'd had this conversation before."

"Have we? Ah, now you've brought it to my attention, I think you're right. Is this the chap you were seeing after Chris walked out on you?"

"That's right," she replied, her cheeks getting hotter under his probing gaze.

"And you're now living together?"

"We are. He moved in last month."

"With his dog?"

"It's complicated. This is a new pup."

"New pup, or shouldn't I ask?"

Sam wished the floor would open up and draw her to that elusive abyss. She detested her love life and living arrangements being the topic of their discussion. When it was her boss asking the questions, how the heck could she squirm her way out of this one?

"No matter. It wasn't my intention to pry. I can see I'm causing you some discomfort."

Sam waved her hand, dismissing his observation. "It's fine. Deep down I'm quite a private person."

He gave her a reassuring smile. "I can take a hint. Do you need a hand with the case? Is everyone on your team pulling their weight?"

"Oh yes, I have no qualms there. To be honest, it's too early to tell if I will need to throw more resources at the investigation. Can I get back to you later?"

"Of course you can. I can see I'm hampering your progress. Call me if and when you need any further assistance. Don't be shy, okay?"

"You have my word, sir. Thank you for dropping by, I'll keep you updated."

"Please do. TTFN."

With that, he breezed out of the room, and Sam closed her eyes and let out the biggest sigh she'd exhaled in a very long time. The thought of him stripping her and the team of the investigation had rocked her world. Every police officer of her calibre would feel the same if they had that kind of threat hanging over their heads.

Seconds later, a knock sounded on the door.

"Yes, what is it?" Sam shouted, annoyed and keen to get on with her day without further interruptions.

Bob poked his head around the door. "Umm... I thought I'd better check, see if you were all right."

"Why? Shouldn't I be? So what if the boss dropped by to see me? It doesn't always mean that I've been pulled over hot coals, you know."

Bob stared at her, his mouth gaping open at her swift, harsh retort. "Pardon me for caring. I'll leave you alone in that case."

Sam let out a guttural groan. "No, don't. I'm sorry. Come in."

"Do you want to do this over a fresh cup of coffee?"

Sam smiled. "You say all the right things... occasionally."

"Yeah, when it suits, eh? I'll be back in a tick."

While he was gone, she sourced Jackie Penrose's number, ready for when her partner left again, to organise a press conference to take place at her earliest convenience. First, she needed to get her best grovelling gene primed and ready for action.

Her partner drifted back into the room a few seconds later, carrying two cups of steaming coffee. He handed one to Sam and took a seat. "Want to talk about it?"

"About what? You're going to need to be more specific if your intention is for me to be more forthcoming about what's going on in my head at the moment."

"I see, it's going to be one of those types of conversations, is it?"

Sam rolled her eyes. "What type of conversations? You've lost me, not for the first time."

"It probably won't be the last either. Aren't we supposed to be partners? I thought partners assisted each other when they're struggling."

She shook her head. "You're reading too much into this, as usual. Had this conversation taken place at six-thirty last night then you might have a case for thinking that way."

"Okay. What about the boss? Was he giving you gyp?"

"Not really. He'd heard about the investigation and voiced his concerns."

"Am I supposed to know what that means?"

"Leave it, Bob. All you need to know is that I'm handling things. Granted, I might not be working on all cylinders at present, but that will pass."

Bob shrugged, rose from his seat and walked towards the door. "Let me know when you feel like sharing."

Her irritation spiked and she wondered why she was always prickly with him, how he had the ability to annoy her for even the slightest things. "I will."

He left the room and closed the door firmly behind him. Sam took the next few seconds to clear her mind and get the investigation back on track.

She rang Jackie Penrose. "Hi, Jackie, it's Sam Cobbs."

"Hey, Inspector, how are things going for you this week?"

"Don't ask. I'm after a favour."

"You need me to call a press conference ASAP, right?"

"Am I that predictable?"

"Put it this way, the only reason you ring me is to request a press conference."

"Ah yes, that's true. Sorry. What are the chances of it happening today?"

"You're in luck. I have a slot already booked for three this afternoon. Another inspector requested it but has since caught the perpetrator so no longer has any use for it. I was about to call it off. What do you say?"

"That would be great, thanks so much."

"Is this the case I've been hearing rumours about?"

"Gosh, I suppose. I've just had my DCI in here asking about it. Apparently, I'm the talk of the station."

"Aww... not in that sense, Sam. People are concerned about you, that's all. How are you holding up?"

"I've had better days, make that weeks. But I'm plodding on. It's what we women do, isn't it? No one's going to chip in and do our work for us, are they?"

"That's the spirit. You know where I am if you ever feel the need to unload your troubles. I can be very discreet."

"Thanks, I'll bear it in mind. I've got to fly. I'll see you downstairs at about five to three."

"Looking forward to it. Take care, Sam."

"Thanks, you, too."

Sam ended the call, and rather than dwell on what Jackie had said, put her head down and cracked on with her mundane task of going through the post and her emails until her mind went numb and she needed a breather. She left the office and called out, "Anyone want a top-up?"

Claire and Bob both nodded. Sam poured the coffee and deposited the cups on each of their desks. She lingered beside Bob and shuffled her feet.

"Did you need something, boss?" he asked, his gaze locked on his computer screen.

"To apologise," she mumbled, loud enough only for him to hear. "I just need a little space to sort my head out, Bob."

"Why didn't you just say that? I'll give you all the space you need."

"Thanks. Back to business… Have you heard from the others?"

"Not since they set off. I suppose it's too early yet."

"Okay, I thought as much. I have a few notes to make. There's a press conference happening at three this afternoon."

"Good job. Let's hope someone out there can throw us a lifeline before we start drowning."

Sam laughed. "Ever the optimist, eh? I'll be in my office." She took her cup and returned to her seat, choosing to ignore the rest of the unopened brown envelopes sitting in her in-tray.

Twenty minutes later, and with her notes all up to date and her statements from last night loaded into files, she returned to the outer office to find Claire on the phone.

"I'll pass the message on, okay, Suzanna, take care." Claire ended the call and said, "They've found a witness who saw a man wearing a hood leave the park and get into a dark car."

Sam's adrenaline flowed. "Anything more than that? Reg number, make and model perhaps?"

"Sadly not. The witness said he was distracted, his dog wasn't well, he was comforting it in the back of the car. He happened to glance up and saw this man swiftly leaving the park. He didn't think anything of it at the time."

"Something is better than nothing, I suppose," Bob said.

"I guess," Sam said. "Let's hope the door-to-door enquiries throw some extra details into the mix."

Bob ran his hand through his hair. "Maybe the response from the press conference will prove beneficial this time around."

"Talking of which, I should make a move," Sam said. "I won't be too long, hopefully."

"Depends if the journalists go easy on you or not," Bob said.

Sam held up her crossed fingers and dipped back into her office to collect her notes.

AFTER THE CONFERENCE had ended and the journalists had dispersed, Jackie took Sam to one side to check if she was okay.

"Don't worry about me, I'm fine. Getting better by the hour. What's that saying? Ah, yes, you can't keep a good woman down."

"Make sure you get some rest tonight, Sam. This will be aired on the evening news, as usual. The calls probably won't filter through until later this evening or first thing in the morning."

"I'll see if one of the team is up for some overtime. Thanks for all your help, Jackie."

"You're welcome, as always. Good luck. Glad to see you're on the mend now and not letting this affect you so much."

"I have good people around me, keen to point out the error of my ways." Sam grinned and made her way back upstairs to the incident room.

The rest of the team had all arrived back. Sam spoke to them individually to see what they'd established, if anything. Suzanna told her that she and Liam had visited the school. The headmistress and her team were all shocked to hear the news but couldn't give them any insight into what might have been going on in Amelia's life as she was regarded as a fairly private person. Nothing had come up at school during the working week that anyone was willing to throw into the mix.

Sam's heart sank when she heard that news. "It looks like we're going to be reliant on what the conference brings in then. Anyone up for a bit of overtime, manning the phones tonight?"

Liam raised a tentative hand in the air. "I'll have to check with Sarah first, but I don't mind hanging around, boss, especially if it gets me out of trawling through dozens of wedding brochures again."

Sam cringed. "Okay, check with Sarah. I wouldn't want to be responsible for you two falling out, not this close to the wedding."

"Yeah, that's just it, we get married next month, and she's still finding things we need to order. Anyone would think we're made of money. I keep pleading with her to rein it in but…"

"She wants it all for her big day, eh? I feel for you. Weddings are getting more and more expensive every year. Make the call and get back to me, Liam."

He picked up his mobile off his desk and jabbed at a number and then left the room to speak to Sarah out in the hallway. He returned, red-faced, a few minutes later. "All set, boss."

"What? No aggro?"

"Oh, there was plenty of that, but I slapped her down and told her the overtime would come in handy. She relaxed a bit then. I could hear the cogs churning into life at the prospect of having an extra few quid to spend."

"Oh dear, life is tough at times, Liam. Anyway, thanks for volunteering. Work until ten-thirty then call it a day."

"Suits me, boss. All right if I nip out and grab something to eat before you head off home?"

"Go for it."

Sam brought the whiteboard up to date and then circled the room again before she told everyone to go home for the evening. It wasn't until she'd uttered those words that the exhaustion hit her.

Bob appeared beside her. "You've done well today," he whispered.

"Thanks. Let's all go home and get some rest. I've got a feeling we're going to be run off our feet tomorrow."

"Really? You think we're going to get a lot of joy from the press conference?"

"Either that or something else. I'm having trouble putting my finger on it, but there's a definite feeling in my gut that is hard to shift."

"I suppose time will tell. Any plans for this evening?"

"I was going to say a spot of dog walking at the park but

I think we might take them for a ride and go elsewhere for a while. Not sure I could face going back there again, not yet."

"Understandable. There must be plenty of walks in your area, now that the nights are lighter. That's got to be in your favour."

"Yeah. Don't worry, Rhys and I will sort something out. Have a good evening, Bob. Say hi to Abigail and the girls for me."

"I'll do that."

She patted Liam on the shoulder on her way out. "Ring me if anything significant comes to light this evening."

"I'll do that, boss. Have a good one."

Sam racked her brains for somewhere else suitable to walk the dogs on the way home. She rang Rhys at six. "Hi, are you at home yet?"

"Not far. Don't tell me you're working late."

"I'm not. I'm trying to figure out where to take the dogs for their constitutionals."

"Leave it with me, I've been doing some research in between clients today. Want me to collect Sonny from Doreen?"

"That would be wonderful, thanks. See you in around ten minutes." She ended the call and then stretched out her neck and eased it round in a circle to get rid of the tension in her muscles.

Rhys met her with the two dogs outside the house. She made a quick fuss of them and asked, "Where are we going?"

"I'm going to take us on a magical mystery tour. Do you need to change your shoes?"

"I've got it covered, my wellies are in the boot."

. . .

An hour later, with the dogs exercised and ready for their dinner, they entered the house, and Sam raided the fridge for something to eat. "Pasty and chips, do you?"

"I haven't had one of those in years. Sounds good to me. Anything I can do?"

"Feed the dogs and lay the table for me, if you will?"

"Consider it done. Nice walk. Made a change to go somewhere new."

"It was spot on. We'll have to search for more secret paths like that. It wasn't too muddy in the end."

After they had eaten dinner, Sam excused herself to check in with Liam. "Anything yet, Liam?"

"Not a single call, ma'am. I think it's going to be a long night. Do you need me to do anything rather than sitting here twiddling my thumbs?"

"Not really. Check all the files are up to date on the last few cases we've solved, other than that, I think we're on top of everything."

"Makes a change. Sod's law, right?"

"Yep. Don't stay any longer than ten-thirty."

"I won't. Enjoy the rest of your evening, boss."

"I'd say the same to you, except…"

They both laughed, and Sam hung up. Rhys presented her with a glass of wine, and they cuddled up on the sofa with Casper and Sonny wedged between them.

"I don't usually like to watch myself on the TV," she said, "but do you mind?"

"I was about to suggest the same. What's it like? In front of the camera?"

"Nerve-racking at times. I'm surprised my mouth doesn't dry up."

"It would be the same for me. Another reason I admire you so much."

She leaned over to kiss him. "Why, thank you, kind sir. It depends on the day and if the journalists behave or not."

"And if they don't? Do you have their cards marked?"

Sam chuckled. "Not in that respect. But I tend to dodge their questions during the next few conferences."

"That's my girl. Are you any further forward with the case?"

"No, that's the frustrating part. The door-to-door enquiries proved to be disappointing, so we're going to be reliant on what the press conference throws up. The major disadvantage we have is that the murder took place in my community which is relatively small, so the likelihood of someone being in the right place at the right time is minimal."

"Ah, I can see that. Where do you go from here, if nothing is forthcoming from the conference?"

"I wish someone would tell me. Right now, I haven't got a clue."

CHAPTER 3

It was hard to shift the feeling of doom hanging over Sam as she drove into work the following day. Liam had contacted her on his way home the previous evening and reported that in the end, there was nothing actually to report. Now she was left wondering in which direction to turn next, to get the investigation started.

She bypassed the coffee-making area and went straight into her office to knuckle down to her post. Halfway through, she paused to look at a handwritten white envelope. Instinct told her to handle it carefully, and she snapped on a pair of gloves before she opened it.

Inside was a typed note that was signed *Changer of Lives*. The note read:

I swooped, took what I wanted, and then left her there to die. Her Maker will receive her; she won't be missed here.

. . .

Dozens of questions bombarded her mind. How did the note appear on her desk? Did the perpetrator drop it off at reception by hand? Would the cameras have picked up the perpetrator? Why contact her? Yes, she was in charge of the case, but usually criminals did all they could to avoid making contact with her, so why is this perpetrator different? Was he gloating? Shoving it down her neck that he'd killed Amelia and that she hadn't got a clue where to start searching for the murderer?

A knock sounded on the door.

"Come in, Bob."

The door opened. "Hey, how did you know it was me?"

She grinned. "Lucky guess." She opened her top drawer and withdrew a pair of gloves. "Put those on."

She threw them across the table. Frowning, he inserted his hands into the gloves. "Why am I doing this?"

"You'll see soon enough."

She handed him the note, and he read it, shaking his head and tutting in the process.

"Fuck, he's got some nerve, sending this to you. Want me to get it over to the lab?"

"We'll do it later. Do you think he targeted her on purpose?"

"It seems pretty personal to me. Effing warped shit. Fancy him sending you a note. He's one of those creepy fuckers who enjoy toying with the senior officer in charge of a case. We've met his sort a few times over the years, yet to me, a bastard who has got one over on you, though."

"Yes, I thought the same. Still, at least he's made contact with us. That's a good thing. Perhaps he's been sloppy and left half a dozen prints all over the paper or envelope."

"You reckon? My take is he's probably got more brains than to do anything as slack as that."

"I'll get it sent to the lab."

"Want me to run a copy off and get that organised for you? I could even whisk it over there myself."

"No, it's fine. We'll swing by the lab when we're out and about. They're probably snowed under anyway, so another couple of hours' delay isn't going to make a difference. By what the killer said, do you think he knew her?"

"It's hard not to think along those lines. What did he mean, she won't be missed?"

Sam shrugged. "After speaking with her husband and mother, I got the impression her marriage was a happy one. There was talk of them trying for a baby soon. You don't tend to do that if you're in an unhappy marriage, do you?"

"Nope. This case is frustrating with a capital F and from right out of the traps, too."

"Yep, you've got that right. And with no bloody calls coming in from the appeal I put out last night, I only think things are going to get a darn sight worse before they get better. What are we missing? Shout out if you think I've brushed over something that I should have highlighted to the team."

"You know me, I would definitely say something. The only positive I can see going for us at the moment is the fact that he's made contact with you. All right, it could be perceived as him gloating, but you have to question why he's got in touch."

"Judging by what we've dealt with in the past, the killers who have had insecurity issues, maybe that's the case with this fucker. Either way, I hope he maintains contact with us because it means he'll hopefully slip up in the near future and it will lead to his arrest."

"Hmm… he must have seen the press conference last night, mustn't he? Otherwise, he wouldn't have known whom to send the note to, right?"

"That's logical. If he hand-delivered it, then we need to

check the CCTV cameras near the main entrance, see if we can catch him on tape."

"I'll check with the desk sergeant, he should know."

"Tell him to keep vigilant and to rig up an extra camera aimed at the post box."

"I'll get on it now. Are you all right about this? The killer getting in touch, I mean?"

"Yeah, I'm fine. I'm determined to catch this bastard. Leaving Amelia alive and in that state was one of the cruellest acts I've ever come across. Why not kill her outright and be done with it?"

"Yeah, heartless. Makes you wonder what goes on in a mind as warped as that."

"Hopefully, it'll be detrimental to his agenda."

"I hope you're right. I'll go and see what Nick has to say." He left the room and popped back a few seconds later. "I've run off a couple of copies and tucked the original letter in an evidence bag."

Sam grinned. "Mr Super-efficient today, aren't you?"

"I can be, if you give me the chance to be. You need to delegate more, I'm always telling you to do it."

"I know. It's hard to let go. It's nothing personal. I think most inspectors work the same way."

"I doubt if that's true, from what I hear on the grapevine."

"Shame on them. I bet they're male." She raised a hand. "No, don't answer that, I'm shocked such a sexist comment came out of my mouth."

He laughed. "I'm not, and you're right, it happens to be the truth."

Sam gave him one of her looks. "There you go! It's the way of the world."

"If you say so. Don't expect me to side with you, you know, what with me being a male."

"Point taken."

He closed the door behind him, and she glanced down at a copy of the note he'd given her. She stared at it long and hard until the letters blurred.

What's your game, Changer of Lives? Did you know Amelia? Or was she someone you bumped into down at the park and chose her as your first victim? Is she your first victim? Or are there others out there, waiting to be discovered? Or is she the first of many? That's usually how these things go. The body count rising swiftly, when some menace, such as yourself, gets out of control. Hangs on to the lust, the thrill of taking someone's innocent life.

So many questions she was dying to put to the perpetrator, but first, they would need to capture him, find out who they were after and haul his arse in to interview. Any chance of doing that were very slim, bordering on the impossible scale with what they had to work with.

Sam decided to make a call to the lab, have a word with Des about the developments in the case so far. She dialled his mobile instead. "Hi, Des, can you talk? It's Sam Cobbs."

"Ah, there you are. I was just about to type up my report and send it over to you. Is something wrong?"

"Plenty. The world has gone nuts. Where do you want me to start?"

"Umm... okay, here's an idea, why don't we keep this relevant for now, what with time never being on our side, and stick with the investigation?"

"Very wise, you clarifying that."

"It has been said that I'm a wise old fool when I want to be."

"Not so much of the old. Do you want to give me a hint on what the PM highlighted, apart from the obvious, that her throat was cut?"

"She was also raped, sexually assaulted, whichever way you want to say it."

"Shit!" Sam threw her pen across the room. "Didn't that

poor woman suffer enough at the hands of this fucking no-mark? To leave her lying there, still alive after cutting her like that?"

"I can tell you're still very upset about this, Sam. Are you sure it's not going to affect your capabilities, dealing with the investigation?"

"No, if anything, it has reinforced my decision to go ahead and solve this case. This bastard needs to be caught. Ah yes, you should know something, the reason behind my call today."

"I'm listening. Can you make it quick? I have another two PMs lined up today, and you know what that means, another late night with two urgent reports to type up and send to the SIOs."

"Sorry, I didn't mean to hold you up. I'll be dropping by the lab later with a letter I need Forensics to go over with a fine-tooth comb."

"A letter, eh? So, he's going to lead you a merry dance, right?"

"Seems that way. He's calling himself 'Changer of Lives'."

"The sick fucker. By that I take it he's going to strike again, if he hasn't already."

"If any suspicious deaths land on the table, will you give me a shout?"

"You'll be at the very top of the list. Now I'm going to have to go, unless you need anything else from me."

"I don't. Saying that, you could chase up Forensics for me in a day or two."

"There will be no need. When you drop the note off, tell them I asked them to make it a priority."

Sam smiled. "Thanks, Des. Enjoy the rest of your day."

"I doubt it very much, but thanks anyway."

He hung up, and Sam replaced her mobile in her jacket pocket and stood. She entered the incident room at the same time as Bob came in the other door. "How did you get on?"

"The sergeant is going to trawl through the footage for us. He said the letter was already in the box when he arrived at about six this morning."

"Interesting. So the perp must have seen the appeal go out last night, got himself worked up about it and written the note then probably dropped it off in the early hours of the morning."

Bob shrugged. "If you say so. Who's to say how things panned out with this bastard? Let's hope he didn't go out on the prowl again, in search of another victim at the same time, if he was that worked up about the appeal."

Sam sighed. "I just spoke to Des. He mentioned he had another two PMs to perform today but didn't hint that the victims died in suspicious circumstances. I've told him about the note and asked him to contact me if any suspicious deaths come his way in the near future."

"Sounds like a plan to me. What now?"

"We'll take the note over to the lab, get that out of the way first and then... well, I haven't got that far yet."

CHAPTER 4

He was out again, on the tail of yet another victim. Sam Cobbs had wound him up when he'd seen her on the screen the previous evening, hence the need to send her a note. However, writing that note and taking the risk to deliver it himself to the station had far from satisfied the desire within him. If anything, it had ignited yet another urge to go on the kill once more.

He hunkered down in his car that he'd parked next to hers. You see, he knew the new victim, had taken a fancy to her when she had shown up during his latest workout at the gym where he trained. He'd tried to start a conversation with her, but Sophie had snubbed him. Actually, she'd looked him up and down and turned her back on him, her disgust blatantly obvious. Well, she'd pay for her bitchy behaviour.

A noise alerted him, tearing him out of his reverie. She was on the steps of the gym, laughing with a couple of her friends. They drifted off, and she came his way, towards her car. He sat there, his heart pounding, sensing she wasn't about to go with him willingly. She was fit, so the likelihood of her putting up a fight was off the scale. He would be ready for every trick she pulled. It was obvious how feisty she was going to be. He glanced at the passenger seat and surveyed the items he had laid out beside him. The gaffer tape would be his first choice. And then the black bag would be used to suppress her. That and a swift right hook. He definitely wasn't opposed to using brute strength to achieve his ambition.

She got closer to her car door. They were out of range of the nearest streetlight. He watched her indicators light up as she pressed the key fob to open the doors. His hand lingered over the handle, ready to jump out. She dumped her gym bag in the boot and grabbed a bottle of water which she opened alongside him. He waited until she reached for the door handle, then he did the same and leapt out of the car. She was too wrapped up in her thoughts to notice him. He struck her, one cracking clout to the jaw with his shaking clenched fist, and she dropped to the ground. Not out cold, just sitting there, dazed. He dipped back into his car and tore off a strip of tape that he secured across her mouth.

Sophie, realising what was happening, put up a fight. She kicked out, catching him in the shin a couple of times.

"Bitch, you'll pay for that, you'll see."

She bit something back at him, but the tape did its job of quelling her words. He laughed and gathered her wrists in his large hand then tied a piece of rope around them.

Sophie thrashed her head from side to side and bashed him with her fists. He took a step back and stared at her. Then he kicked her thigh and warned, "Shut the fuck up, or there will be more where that came from. You and I are going to take a drive now. I have a cosy cottage out in the middle of nowhere lined up, somewhere we're going to get more acquainted."

Muffled cries emerged, and he hit her again. This time, he rendered her unconscious and had no problem picking her up and bundling her into the boot of his car. It would be a bumpy ride for her in there, and the smell from the oily rags he'd used at the weekend to carry out an oil change would no doubt piss her off. That was down to her, she should have been more compliant with his wishes.

An hour later, and he drew up outside the cottage he'd borrowed from a mate of his. Wayne Powell had only had it a few months, mainly visited the place when the weather was fine at the weekends and he fancied a walk up on the fells. Garner unlocked the door and swiftly looked around to see what was on offer. Not a lot, it was the definition of basic in his eyes.

"Oh well, needs must. It'll only be for a few days."

Garner returned to the car and flicked the catch on the boot. Sophie stared up at him, cowering, her eyes wide with fear.

"Come now, there's really no need for you to be scared of me."

He held out his hand to help her out of the boot. But she shuffled back under the shelf and shook her head.

"You'd better reconsider, and quickly. You wouldn't want to see me lose my temper now, would you?"

She backed further under the shelf, and he lost it. He gripped her bound wrists and wrenched them towards him. Then he grappled with her legs that he'd mistakenly left free of any bindings and tugged her out of the car. In the process, he accidentally slammed her hip against the catch of the boot. She cried out.

He laughed. "You try to continue to resist, and there will be more where that came from, I can assure you. Now, are you going to behave? Or do you want more of the same?"

She stood there in front of him, staring right through him, her eyes blazing with hatred.

"That's what I thought. Get inside."

He shoved her towards the front door. Her head swivelled to each side. He was aware of what she was doing. She was taking in her surroundings, undoubtedly weighing up an escape route if the opportunity arose.

"Don't even think about it. I've got a large knife inside and I'll slit your throat with it before you manage to get two feet away from me. You'd be wise to remember that, too."

Once inside the cottage, he secured the door with the key which he placed in his jacket pocket, again, under her watchful gaze. He laughed, tipping his head back. "You're a fool if you think I can't read what's going on in that pretty little head of yours." He forced her towards the sofa over to the right and pushed her onto it. "Coffee? I'm having one."

He ripped the tape off her mouth, and she cried out.

"No, stick your coffee and anything else you have on offer. I want nothing from you."

"We'll see. We're going to be here for a while. I'm guessing you'll change your mind, eventually."

"Screw you, mister. What do you want from me?"

"You'll find out soon enough."

He lowered his head towards hers, and she headbutted him.

He stumbled backwards, stunned. Then he sprang forward, gripped her by the throat and sneered, "You'll regret that later."

She spat at him. "Fuck off, dickhead! I've got no intention of giving in to you. I'll fight you every step of the way, you're going to have to kill me."

"Don't worry, it's on the cards. Your end may come to fruition sooner than you think."

Her eyes narrowed into tiny slits. "Bring it on, fucker, I

have a few tricks up my sleeve to deal with morons like you."

He sniggered. "Thanks for the warning. I had an inkling that you'd be well up on your self-defence."

"Shit, I've just realised where I know you from."

He raised an eyebrow. "I've never tried to disguise my identity from you, which usually means one thing."

"Yeah, bring it on. I knew you were a creep the minute I laid eyes on you down at the gym."

"You shouldn't have treated me the way you did. It was your downfall, lady."

"Whatever. Creeps like you need to know their place in this world. Is this the only way you can get a girl's attention? By kidnapping her and keeping her restrained? Wow, what a sad individual you are. I did the right thing, avoiding you at the gym."

"No, you didn't, it was your demise, if you must know. You women make me sick. You go to these gyms only to flutter your eyelids at the muscle-bound goons down there. The likes of me don't get a look-in, do they?"

"Scumbags like you, you mean. There's a difference."

"Whatever. Do you want a drink or not?"

She contemplated the question for a few more seconds and then finally nodded. "Yes."

He went back out to the car and fetched the shopping bag from the back seat. After unloading it and putting away the essentials he had brought with him, he filled the kettle and prepared two mugs he removed from the cupboard above his head. "Milk and sugar? I'm guessing neither, not with a figure like that."

"Neither."

He nodded smugly. He knew he was right, he could read her sort like a book. He looked at the view out of the window, the mountains surrounding them, and pondered what his next move should be while the kettle boiled. He caught a reflection of Sophie in the corner of the window and appraised her every move. She was busy weighing the place up, just like she'd done outside. He poured the water in the mugs, added milk and sugar to his and crossed the room to the seating area. He placed her drink in front of her on the low coffee table.

"You're going to need to untie my hands to allow me to drink," she said, her tone as contemptable as the look she was giving him.

"You can manage. Stop trying to pull a fast one, it won't wash with me, Sophie."

"I'm not. How do you know my name?"

He laughed and pulled up a dining chair and sat opposite her. "It didn't take much. A word in the right ear, and a few of the members were quite forthcoming about you down at the gym. That's why I was surprised at you turning me down." It was all a lie, but it worked well for him.

"What utter bullshit. You're a screwed-up fucking moron coming out with such rubbish."

"Am I? Why's that then?"

"Why?" It was her turn to laugh. "Because I'm frigging gay and I'm married… to a bloody woman. How wrong can one man be? You twisted fucking shit. I'm *gay!*"

He was taken aback by her revelation. Her reasons for rejecting him had never even crossed his mind. "Why go to the gym, if not to latch on to one of the fellas down there?"

"Jesus! Are you for real? Gyms are places where people go when they're doing their best to keep fit. They are not where saddos hang out to pick up a date. Oh, wait, you're the exception to the rule. What a messed-up fucker you are."

He flew out of his seat and gripped her around the throat, cutting off the air to her windpipe. She grasped at his hands, trying to loosen his grip as she choked.

"Stop putting me down, you condescending bitch. You

need to understand the dire straits you're in and stop driving me to my limits. I'll only take so much before I snap. You really don't want to know what the consequences would be if I did that."

He released his grip, and she gasped, then sucked in some deep breaths to recover the air he'd cut off.

Garner returned to his seat, and they stared at each other, neither of them saying another word until they'd both calmed down.

"You need to realise the words that tumble out of your mouth will have consequences."

She shook her head in defiance. "Kill me, you might as well get it over and done with."

He laughed. "Where would the fun be in doing that? Gay or not, I'm about to have some fun with you, bitch."

Her mouth twisted in anger, and her nose wrinkled in disgust. "Touch me, and it'll be the last thing you do." She picked up her cup of steaming-hot coffee and aimed it at him.

His chair tipped backwards in his eagerness to escape. He bounced back onto his feet before she had a chance to move. He was on her in a flash. Pinning her down and taking advantage of her. Dishing out his punishment the only way he knew how. When it was over, she lay there, sobbing, tears mixing with the blood on her face from the cuts she'd received during her ordeal.

She should have given in to his demands. Instead, she'd chosen to fight him every step of the way, resisting the inevitable outcome.

"You should have complied with my wishes and not wound me up."

"You disgust me. Why don't you kill me and be done with it?"

"Because bitches like you need to be taught a lesson.

Where would the fun be in ending it all quickly?"

"You won't come near me again. I won't let you."

He openly laughed in her face. "You want to bet?"

She cowered away from him and hid her face in the cushion.

He left her there to sob. He'd come back to her soon enough. He had strategies to fulfil, people he needed to contact. But before he could surge forward with his plans, he'd need to secure his hostage. He went out to the car again and retrieved another length of rope from the front seat and his laptop from the footwell on the passenger side of his car. When he returned, Sophie was missing.

Frantically, he searched every room in the cottage. She was nowhere to be seen. He tried the back door and found it unlocked, with the key still in it. He kicked himself for being such a fool and took off after her. She couldn't be far, a few meters ahead of him, that's all, surely. In the distance he heard a noise and, craning his neck and ear, he soon figured out what it was.

"Shit!" He tore back to the cottage just in time to see his car disappearing out of sight. She must have inched her way around the front of the cottage when he'd taken off after her.

He bolted after the car, successfully getting his bearings, and with the light now fading, he changed directions and sped off through the trees, heading for the main road. She wouldn't have a clue which direction to head in, she was a woman after all, they rarely had any sense of direction. The car was coming towards him. He stood in the middle of the road, guessing that she wouldn't have the nerve or guts to hit him. He was wrong. She put her foot down and came hurtling straight at him. He had picked up a rock and hurled it at the windscreen. She took her hands off the steering wheel to shield her face as the rock flew towards her. The car veered off the road and straight into a tree.

CHAPTER 5

Two days later

"Morning, ma'am. How are you on this wonderful bright morning?" Nick asked as soon as Sam entered the main entrance to the station.

She glanced over her shoulder at the mist descending in the car park and then gave him a quizzical look. "Am I missing something, or have you finally lost the plot, young man?"

He tried to suppress a giggle but failed. "Sorry, you know me too well to keep up the pretence any longer. I was hoping to have a quick word with you on your way through, if you have the time?"

"As it happens, I haven't."

His face dropped, and she broke into a smile.

"Just kidding. What's up? Want to do it here?"

"Somewhere more private, if you don't mind, ma'am."

Sam opened the door to the small reception office where

they held discreet interviews with members of the public who requested a bit of privacy. He followed her into the room, closed the door behind him and cleared his throat.

"Is this a serious matter, Nick? Is it personal?"

"No, sorry if I'm dithering and giving you the wrong impression, it's just that… this isn't sitting comfortably with me."

"What isn't?"

"A woman came into the station at seven this morning, and, well…"

Sam flicked her sleeve back and looked at her watch. "Time's getting on, and I'd rather not be late, if it's all the same to you, Nick."

"Sorry, bloody hell, what's got into me? I'm a blithering idiot, standing here like a teenager on his first date."

Sam couldn't resist letting out a laugh. "It's now my turn to apologise. I shouldn't laugh. Come on, come right out with it, the anticipation is killing me."

"Right, okay. Well, the thing is, this woman, she came in here and was beside herself. I sat her down with a nice cup of tea and persuaded her to tell me what was wrong."

"And?"

"At first, she was too embarrassed to tell me. Said that society had always treated her and her sort differently. It took me a while to work out what she meant, and then she showed me a photo that she kept in her purse, of her and another woman."

Sam frowned and inclined her head. "What are you telling me? That she's gay?"

"Yes, she's a lesbian and was too embarrassed, maybe even a little ashamed, to admit it openly. Can you believe it, in this bloody day and age?"

"All right, now with the fact established, would you mind telling me why she sought out our help in the first place? Has someone physically assaulted her because of her sexual preferences?"

"Not exactly. She was here to report her *wife* as a missing person."

Sam held a hand to her face. "Jesus… I see where you're coming from now. Did she say how long her wife had been missing?"

"Two days. She knew that we wouldn't be interested in her filing a report until the first twenty-four hours were up, but when it came to the crunch, she struggled to come down here at all. In the end, a friend of hers persuaded her that she would be letting down her other half if she didn't report her missing."

"Really? The poor woman sounds very confused and, while I feel sorry for her, I'm not sure why this has anything to do with me, Nick. Care to enlighten me?"

"Here's the thing. You know as well as I do when something doesn't sit right with you, ma'am. I'm getting a sense that this case could be connected to the murder inquiry you're dealing with at the moment."

"What? How can you say that?"

He clenched his fist and held it over his stomach. "I can't give you any more than that, it's a gut feeling. I know it sounds bizarre and I'm asking you to go out on a limb for me with this one, but would you at least have a word with the woman, if only to appease me and help me get rid of this ominous sensation in my gut?"

Sam tutted and rolled her eyes. "Go on then, just for you. I wouldn't do this for anyone else."

Nick beamed, and she followed him out of the room.

"I'll be forever grateful to you. Let me get the woman's details for you now."

"I'll need to check in with the team first. Once I've done

that, I'll call round and see the woman. The question is, am I likely to get any sense out of her?"

"Once I'd managed to coerce the information out of her, she appeared to be more at peace with herself."

"It's hard to imagine someone being that insecure about the choices they make that they're willing to brush their partner's absence under the carpet."

"I think you'll understand more about her reasoning once you get to meet her, ma'am." He handed her a slip of paper which she tucked into her jacket pocket.

"Thanks. I'd better get on with my day. I should be ready to head off in the next thirty minutes or so."

"Appreciate it, ma'am, I truly do."

Sam smiled and punched in her code which allowed her through the security door and into the inner sanctum. She climbed the stairs in a world of her own and neglected to see DCI Armstrong standing at the top. He appeared to be waiting for her.

"Morning, Inspector Cobbs."

She glanced up and slammed a hand over her racing heart. "Sorry, sir. You caught me daydreaming, kind of. It was to do with the case, I promise."

"Still having issues, are you?" His voice was stern but caring at the same time.

"Not in that respect. It's fine, just planning what lies ahead of us today."

"I see. Okay, any problems, you know where I am." He turned and walked the length of the corridor to his office.

Sam watched him go, all the time wondering if she should have divulged what was really going on in her head. In the end, she decided that she'd done the right thing in keeping quiet, at least until she had all the facts in front of her and things were making more sense in her own mind.

Bob launched out of his seat the second she stepped into the room. "Morning, boss. Coffee?"

"When have you ever known me to say no? We'll have to make it a quick one, you and I need to get on the road pretty soon."

"Oh, may I ask why?"

"I'll fill you in on the way. Will you bring it in for me? I'll give my post a cursory glance just in case the killer has decided to contact me again."

They had gone over the CCTV footage the previous day or so and found nothing. It wasn't until Nick had got in touch that the riddle had been solved about how the killer's note had been delivered. He'd apparently asked one of the constables to accept the letter from him on the edge of the car park. When Sam had questioned the female constable, she'd had trouble identifying the man. She'd been running late for work. He was on a bike and had fallen off in the main road and was nursing a supposedly injured leg. She'd asked if she could help, and he told her that he'd been asked to drop off some information in connection with a case. She had obliged, by taking the envelope from his gloved hand, and the rest was history. So here they were, sitting with an open investigation, not getting very far. Had they been up to their necks in leads then she wouldn't have had any qualms in rejecting Nick's plea.

Nick was a good man, rarely let her down when she asked him and his team for backup, so there's no way she could have ignored his request. She flicked through the letters, and one in particular caught her attention.

Bob entered the room and found her examining the envelope. "Shit! That isn't what I think it is, is it?" He deposited her mug on the table and stood alongside her.

"I recognise the handwriting." Sam extracted a pair of

gloves from her pocket, opened the envelope and carefully removed the letter. "Fuck, it's from him."

Bob inched closer. "What does the bastard have to say this time?"

Hello, DI Cobbs, how is the investigation going? Well, I hope. LOL

Just to inform you that while you were tucked up in your bed a couple of nights ago, I struck again. Don't worry, the lady in question is a guest in my cottage, for now. To know more about my charming, if a little feisty, house guest, you need to be at the post box on Albert Street at five this evening. If you're a no-show, then the woman's life will hang in the balance and the onus will lay at your door.

Again, the letter was typed, even though the envelope was handwritten. "Shit! He was right."

Bob frowned and took a step back to look at her. "He? Who? And what was he right about?"

"Come on, we need to be somewhere. Bag the letter and envelope, we'll drop them over at the lab. No, wait, print off a copy or three first."

"Hey, slow down. You lost me a long time ago. What's going on, Sam?"

"We don't have time for this, not now, Bob. You're going to have to trust me. Just do what I say, we need to get on the road."

Bob hurriedly snapped on a pair of gloves, snatched the letter from her hand and rushed out of the office. Sam tidied up the rest of her post and shoved them back into her in-tray for later.

She joined Bob in the incident room. "I haven't got time

to go into detail right now, guys, but the killer has been in touch with a second note, informing me that he's holding a woman hostage. Bob and I have to nip out for a while. Carry on with the tasks I set you. Claire, have a word with the desk sergeant. The note was hand-delivered again, let's see if we can catch the bugger on the cameras this time. We'll be back soon. Come on, Bob, we haven't got time on our side, not on this one."

He put the copies he'd made on Claire's desk. "Do the necessary with them, Claire. We've got the original, we'll drop it off at the lab while we're out. That's the plan anyway."

"Leave it with me, Bob. Good luck."

Sam and Bob tore down the stairs. Bob had the sense not to bombard Sam with questions during their speedy descent. They entered the reception area, and Nick glanced up from his paperwork to offer up a smile.

Sam looked him in the eye and said three words: "You were right."

He gasped and shouted after her, "If you need a hand with anything, let me know, ma'am."

"Don't worry, I will. Explain later."

Bob kept up with her pace, and they both jumped in the car.

"Are you going to tell me where we're off to and what the hell is going on?"

Sam let out a large breath. "Sorry, let me input the address in the satnav and get on the road first."

"Jesus, there would be hell to pay if I kept you in the dark like this."

"It's not intentional. There, all done. Buckle up, I'm going to be using the siren to get us there swiftly."

"Where? God, I could quite happily wring your neck right now, boss or no boss, female or not. You're driving me to distraction with all this clandestineness, if that's a bloody word."

Sam laughed and left the car park before she hit the siren. "Get you. I'll let you in on a secret: I have no idea if that's a word or not either."

"Sam," he warned.

"All right. When I arrived this morning, Nick had a word with me about a case that has just come his way."

"Why do I sense we're going to get buried in work anytime soon?"

"Hear me out. He was perturbed about the case and put it my way because he trusts his gut."

"Okay. Are you going to tell me what case you're on about here?"

"Give me a chance," Sam replied. She swerved around a painfully slow car in front of her. The driver of a van, travelling in the opposite lane blasted his horn and raised a clenched fist. "Arsehole. No respect these days, even with the blues and twos in full swing."

"Never mind that twat, what about this extra case we're going to be taking on, bearing in mind that the killer has upped the ante already today, sending you that note?"

"I think, we think, Nick and I think, the case he wanted me to delve into is connected with our ongoing investigation."

"You're still not making any sense."

Sam went over how the conversation with Nick had gone first thing that morning, and Bob let out a whistle.

"Ah, I'm with you. Now you believe the woman the killer has abducted could be this woman's wife, is that it?"

Sam nodded. "Bingo. You know I'm not really one for believing in coincidences."

"Gotcha. Shit, and we're going there to break the news to her wife?"

"We'll need to see how the ground lies first. I don't think we should reveal about the note just yet, you know, in case we end up with egg on our faces. We'll sound her out, get the gist of what's going on first and go from there."

"I was going to suggest the same. The killer didn't give the woman's name in the letter, so in theory, he could have kidnapped her anyway, couldn't he?"

"Which is why I said we need to be restrained about putting all our cards on the table, for now."

"Sorry to make you repeat yourself. I'm catching up slowly, you've had longer to process everything."

"I know." Sam continued to swerve in and out of the traffic and switched the siren off when the satnav showed they were a few streets away from the location they were after. "Here we are now. So we go in there, playing it cool, not mentioning the letter, okay?"

"You'll be doing all the talking, like usual, so however you want to play it is fine by me."

Sam smiled and parked the car outside the mid-terraced house. The front garden was full of late flowering tulips in a cluster of tubs that brightened up an otherwise dreary space.

She inhaled a few steadying breaths and knocked on the front door. A woman in her late twenties to early thirties opened it a few moments later. Sam offered up her warrant card for her to study.

"Hello, Mrs Meskill. I'm DI Sam Cobbs, and this is my partner, DS Bob Jones. Would it be all right if we come in and speak with you?"

"Oh yes. Oh no, I didn't think anyone would take me seriously down at the station," she said, nervously tucking a stray hair behind her ear.

"There's no need for you to be nervous. We're only here for a brief chat. Just to go over the finer details with you."

"Do come in. The place could do with a tidy-up. I'm sorry, my mind has been elsewhere for the past couple of days."

"No excuses necessary, I fully understand what torment you must be going through."

"Would you like a drink? I could do with a coffee myself, so it really isn't any bother."

"That would be lovely. Two white coffees with one sugar, thanks."

"Go through to the lounge, first door on the right, I won't be long."

Sam entered the room and took in her surroundings. Hanging on the wall over the fireplace was a photo of two women, both wearing wedding dresses. They looked stunning and very much in love. Sam gestured for Bob to sit beside her on the couch.

Mrs Meskill joined them a few minutes later with a tray holding three mugs. She placed it on a large fabric footstool that the couple used as a coffee table, or so Sam assumed.

"Thanks, that's very kind of you. Why don't you tell us what's going on?"

"I'm Ruby by the way, not sure if I mentioned that or not at the front door."

"You didn't. You can call us Sam and Bob."

"I'm super nervous, so you'll have to take that into consideration."

"Don't be. We're here to help. Why don't you tell us what you know?"

"On Tuesday evening, Sophie went to the gym as usual. I was working late that night at the store; I own a bridal boutique in town."

"You do? My sister owns one, too."

"No, are you Crystal's sister? Presuming we're talking about the only other bridal shop I know in town."

"That's right." Sam had trouble suppressing the guilt

gnawing at her insides for not being in touch with her sister more lately.

"We often do business together. Swap dresses if a client wants a specific design and I haven't got a particular style in stock. She's always coming to my rescue lately. She's a lovely lady."

"Best sister anyone could wish to have. I'll tell her you said hello when I next catch up with her."

"Please do. Anyway, as I was saying, I didn't leave work until gone ten on Tuesday. One of my clients was struggling to get to me during the day for a fitting, and time was running out before her big day. I made arrangements for her to come and see me at nine on Tuesday. The fitting ran on longer than usual, and when I got home, I fully expected Sophie to be here, waiting for me with a glass of wine to hand, to help me unwind, and she was nowhere to be seen."

"Did she have plans herself in the evening?"

"Yes, it was her night to go to the gym. I left it until eleven before I rang her, thinking she might have gone to the pub after her workout with her friends. It wouldn't be the first time. The trouble is, when I rang her, I found her phone was switched off."

"And that's unusual?"

"Yes, she never ignores my calls." Ruby ran a hand through her long black hair. Her fingers caught on a knot at the end and made her wince. "I'm scared something bad has happened to her. I waited and waited then I finally plucked up the courage to report her missing."

"Yes, the desk sergeant told me that. You should have contacted us as soon as the twenty-four hours were up."

Her head dipped. "I know. I couldn't bring myself to do it. All this is new to me."

"All what?"

"Being part of a female couple. We do our best to stay

under the radar. You hear so many horrible tales about how the gay community are treated in society these days, it made me wary. I was torn apart. My friend had to give me a good talking-to before I plucked up the courage to report her missing. I feel cut up about the delay now, especially after speaking to the nice desk sergeant. He was lovely and very open with me. He listened to my complaint without judging me. He was a breath of fresh air. Not everyone treats me like that, not once they know I'm gay."

A lump appeared in Sam's throat. She swallowed it down and said, "I'm sorry you feel that way and have had to deal with trouble over the years. Some people need shooting. I can't abide homophobic or racist behaviour, there's no need for it. Everyone is entitled to live their life the way they want to, no questions asked."

"Thank you. It's reassuring that you feel that way."

"Did you contact the gym?"

"I did. They checked their car park, and that's when they found her car still parked there."

"You mentioned that she might have gone to the pub with her friends. Did you try ringing them?"

"Yes, I rang everyone I could think of. They all told me the same, that Sophie was heading home early that evening. She wanted to get dinner ready for me, knowing that I was working late." She placed her hands over her face and cried.

"Please, don't get upset. We'll do all we can to help you. We're going to need to ask some pretty intrusive questions first, to try and get to the facts."

Ruby glanced up and dried her tears. "Ask what you want, I have no secrets. We lead a simple life. She has her interests, I have mine. She likes going to the gym whereas I prefer to take Jack for a walk." She pointed at a little Jack Russell sitting in a basket close to the fire that Sam hadn't noticed when she'd walked in.

"What a sweetheart. I didn't even know he was there. Unusual for a small dog to be quiet."

"He's depressed. Hasn't been the same since Sophie went missing. He lies in his bed all day. I take him to work with me, and he's the same there. Just lies in his basket, staring out at me. It's a total change of character for him. He usually bounces around here and at the shop, demanding treats from me and my clients. It's as though he knows what's happened to her and is traumatised."

"They are sensitive souls. I have two dogs at home, and they definitely pick up on any bad vibes going on around them."

She nodded, and fresh tears welled up. "I'm as lost as he is without Sophie around. We've been inseparable since we met last year. We got married after a couple of months together. You know when something is right. She's the soulmate I've been searching for all my life."

Sam smiled. She felt the same way about Rhys. "Where did you meet?"

"At a nightclub. We were both out letting our hair down with friends, umm… both celebrating our recent divorces from our husbands."

"Oh, so neither of you…" Sam stopped mid-sentence, fearing her question might be too personal for the woman to cope with at this time.

"I know what you were about to ask, and no, neither of us had been with a woman before we met. I think that's why I feel so unnerved at the moment. All of this is new to me, to us. People's perceptions towards us, once they find out that we're gay, can be indifferent to say the least."

"You have no need to feel awkward where we're concerned, I can assure you. I'm appalled that the public still react this way. Never mind, I'll stop there before I climb up on my soap box. Everyone is different and has a right to lead their life as they want to lead it, without anyone else voicing their opinions or revealing their hatred."

"I agree with you and, in an ideal world, that would happen. It really doesn't matter to us, like I said, we tend to mix with our own circuit of friends. We feel safer that way."

"I can understand why. Has Sophie had any issues with any co-workers lately?"

"No, nothing like that at all, she would have told me."

"What job does she do?"

"She's a rep for a sportswear company."

"So does that mean she's out on the road a lot?"

"Yes, most days. The odd day she works from the office in Workington. Tuesday was one of those days. She always goes straight to the gym from the office. Fits in her workouts when time allows."

"I see. When did you last speak to her?"

"That morning we had breakfast together and rang each other at lunchtime, as usual. But why would she go off and leave her car at the gym?"

"Could she have gone off with one of her friends?"

"No, they said they bid her farewell on the steps of the gym and went their separate ways. You see, none of this is making any sense, and the more I sit here thinking about it the more puzzled I am about the situation. We love each other, she would never drop contact with me just like that. Therefore, something must have happened to her… something bad."

Sam snuck a glance in Bob's direction. He sensed her looking at him, faced her and gave a slight shrug.

"What's going on? Do you know something?" Ruby was quick to ask.

Sam raised a hand. "Maybe. Something has come to our attention this morning, and it could well be connected with

Sophie's disappearance, however, I need to add a word of caution because it might prove to be a mistake."

"I don't care, if there's an ounce of hope it's connected to why Sophie has gone missing, am I not entitled to know?"

"Yes, but you're going to need to stay calm if I tell you."

"Of course. I can't believe you're saying this, just tell me what you know. I'm going out of my mind with worry here. I have been for nearly two days, and all the time you knew."

"No, that's not true. It's only in the last hour or two that things have slotted into place. We've been working on another investigation all week, getting closer to the criminal who carried out the crime. Anyway, the perp contacted me a few days ago via the post, and this morning I received a second note from him, telling me that he had abducted another woman."

Ruby melted down. She rocked back and forth and cried. "No, I can't believe this. Why? Why take her?"

"We really don't know the ins and outs, or even if it's Sophie he's referring to."

"What did the note say? Has he hurt her? What's his intention with her? Was she kidnapped because she's gay? Stupid question, but I can't think of another reason why someone should take her."

"As I said, we've only learnt about the abduction in the last couple of hours. You spoke to the desk sergeant this morning, and he had a word with me as soon as I got to work. I'll be honest with you, I was in two minds whether to take on your case or not, only because my team are dealing with the other investigation."

"But the note has changed your mind, and now you think this person has Sophie, is that it?" Ruby tore a tissue from the box sitting on the table beside her.

"It does seem likely, although I haven't had time to check through the other missing persons who have been reported this week. Sometimes, as police officers, the need to work on gut instinct overwhelms us."

"And that's what you're getting here?"

"Yes, but not only me, the desk sergeant had an inkling that the two cases might be connected as well, that's why he got me involved first thing this morning."

Ruby fell silent for a second or two while she wrapped the tissue around her fingers. "Okay, if you go down that route, are you going to tell me about the other investigation you're already working on? Are you allowed to do that? Or is it top secret?"

"No, the information is out there in the public domain. I put out an appeal for witnesses to a crime that was committed at the beginning of the week. I was personally involved, in that I found the victim while I was out walking my dogs at the local park."

"Oh my, another woman? What, she had been attacked?"

Sam exhaled a large breath. "Yes, she had been attacked and left for dead."

"Oh my, no. And you discovered her and saved the day. Is the woman all right? No bad injuries?"

Sam shook her head. The images of what she'd had to contend with that night came flooding back and made her eyes water. "I rang for an ambulance, and before they could arrive, the woman died from her injuries."

Ruby gasped. "Oh no, that poor woman. Why? Why was she killed? Did you see the criminal?"

"No, I believe he left the scene before I found the woman."

"How dreadful. No, this can't be happening. Do you know who this person is? Have they given any indication of who they are through these notes? I watch a lot of films and I've seen a few where women have been abducted. Christ, what if this person has got the idea from one of those?"

Sam shrugged. "There's every possibility that's the case.

No, the person has signed the notes as 'Changer of Lives'. They've not hinted whether they are male or female. I think for now, we're going to go along the lines that we're dealing with a male."

"I can't believe what I'm hearing. Why choose Sophie, if that's what has happened? She's such a sweet person. One who tends to bend over backwards to help others. Even last week we nipped into town for a bite to eat, there was a homeless man sitting on the corner with his dog. She spoke to him, asked him if he was all right, and then gave him a tenner. Not long after that, she helped an old lady who was struggling to cross the street. She didn't know these people and yet she went out of her way to help them, to make their lives better in some small way. I was so proud of her. It's not something that I would ever have contemplated doing, but Sophie didn't think twice about it. That's the type of person she is."

"She sounds a wonderful, caring lady. I want to assure you, we're going to do all we can to bring her back to you."

"But how? If you haven't got a clue who the culprit is?"

"Let me worry about that. Will you do me a favour and keep ringing her phone regularly? If he has abducted her then there's a chance she might gain access to her phone at some point. If that happens, will you call me straight away?" Sam took a business card from her pocket and handed it to her.

"I will. What's the next step?"

"The abductor has told me to meet him somewhere this evening. I'll show up at the requested time and do my best to secure Sophie's release... if he has her. There's always going to be that niggling doubt in my mind."

"And mine. I hope he doesn't have her, considering what he did to the other woman. My mind is so screwed up, I don't know what to think or do next."

"I know and appreciate how difficult this situation must be for you. Please try and remain calm, I'm sure it will all come good in the end."

"But at what cost? You've already told me that the first victim died from her horrific injuries. What's to say that won't happen to Sophie?"

Sam nodded. "I can't give you the reassurances you need, all I can tell you is that we're going to do our utmost to ensure Sophie comes back to you safe and well."

"But you can't guarantee it, can you?" Ruby whispered.

"No, like anything in this life, there are no guarantees. However, I can reassure you that one of the top investigative teams in this region are dealing with your wife's case. Have faith in us, that's all I ask."

Ruby smiled warily. "I do, I'd be foolish not to, wouldn't I?"

Sam and Bob rose from their seats, and Ruby showed them back to the front door.

Sam shook her hand and held on to it as she said, "Trust us. We won't let you down."

"Thank you, I think I do. Will you keep me informed?"

"I can't promise to keep in touch daily but I won't forget you, you have my word."

"That's good enough for me. Good luck, I'll keep my phone with me and charged, day and night, just in case."

"Take care. Ring me if she contacts you. Or if anyone else gets in touch regarding your wife's disappearance."

"I'll do that. Nice to meet you, Inspector. I get a good feeling about you."

"I'm glad."

Sam and Bob left the house, and Sam waved at Ruby, who was still standing by the front door, and then slipped into the car.

"I thought you weren't going to mention the note and

being in touch with this criminal," Bob said. He clicked his seat belt into place and looked at her.

"I know but… you were there, I felt she needed some kind of hope to cling on to." Sam started the car and drove back to the station without Bob saying another word.

IT WAS AN EXCEPTIONALLY LONG DAY, waiting for five o'clock to come around. Sam had sent Liam and Oliver ahead of them, to carry out surveillance at the site. Liam had contacted her fifteen minutes before to tell her that no one had been near the post box since they had arrived. Not what she wanted to hear at all.

Now, here she was, with Bob by her side, pulling up alongside the post box at bang on five. They waited in the car until five minutes had passed, but still no one showed up, not that Sam had expected anyone to turn up and risk getting caught.

"Why am I not surprised?" Bob grumbled. He crossed his arms and hunkered down in his seat.

"All right, cut it out. What was I supposed to do, ignore the request? Get a life, Bob."

"All right, so what do we do now?"

"I'm going to get out and have a hunt around, see if he's left another note or maybe a mobile phone to contact him."

"You've been watching too much TV lately, that much is obvious."

"You're getting to be a grumpy old man. I'm surprised Abigail puts up with you."

"Ooo, get you. She has fringe benefits that she appreciates."

Sam held up a hand. "Don't go there. I have enough vile images circulating my mind at present."

"Bloody charming. Right, two heads are better than one,

I'll join you."

"If you have to. I want a thorough search done, not just a quick nosey around and back to the car. If you're up to the task then yes, you can join me, if not, then stay in the car and out of my way."

"Just because this fucker has put you in a foul mood there's no need for you to take it out on me."

"I'm not. All I'm doing is stating facts. We're wasting time." Sam pulled on the handle and shouldered the door open.

They surveyed the area around them, trying to spot anyone who seemed the least bit interested in their arrival. Liam and Oliver were parked up across the street. She had instructed them to remain vigilant and in the car.

A reluctant Bob joined her, and they searched every inch of that post box but found nothing.

"I told you this was going to be a waste of time," Bob mumbled.

"Pack it in and search again, widen the area this time."

"Why? This guy has got you wrapped around his little finger, toying with you in other words."

"Stop it, Bob. The negativity emanating from you is pissing me off. Are you forgetting there is a woman's life at risk here and that this person has already killed one woman? What the hell am I supposed to do? Ignore him and wait for another body to show up? I would hope you know me well enough to know the likelihood of that happening is zilch."

"Yeah, I know. Ignore me." He circled the post box again and said, "I've got something."

Sam raced to see what he was talking about. Bob pointed at a note taped to the inside of the opening.

"The wind caught it and made it flap, otherwise I would have missed it."

"Good spot. Okay, we'll read it in the car."

They raced back and sat in the vehicle. Sam was already wearing a pair of gloves. She tore open the envelope and read the message aloud. "It sounds like some kind of riddle."

SEEK *what you're searching in the tunnel with one entrance at a location far away from traffic. You have until tomorrow to find her, or she'll die.*

SAM STARTED THE CAR.

"Where are you going?" Bob asked.

"Back to the station. We can all try and figure it out while we study the huge map we have in the incident room. With the team's input, between us, we should have this nailed down soon."

"You reckon? Not from that clue. But hey, I've never been a logical thinker."

"You don't say," Sam retorted, her tone laced with sarcasm. "Contact the team, tell them what the plan is."

Ten minutes later, the four of them entered the incident room, and while Bob dished out the coffees to the team, Sam brought the others up to date.

"Any ideas, guys? A tunnel with one entrance, what could that be?"

"A room, or a place with only one door?" Claire suggested.

Sam shook her head and placed her thumb and finger around her chin. "Not sure about that, Claire. A tunnel is dark, right? So a dark place that only has one entrance? Well, it's foxed me."

"What about a cave?" Alex asked.

Sam's nod gained momentum. "I think he's got it. Now all we have to do is find a suitable location on the map, bearing in mind the other snippet of information he's given us in the clue."

Bob shifted to stand in front of the map. "Liam, search the internet for all the names of caves in the area, will you?"

"On it, Bob."

"I can locate at least seven in the area," Liam said. "The first one is past Penrith. No, sorry, make that nine, but there are a few more in the south, too."

"Can you shout out the names and bring up any information you can find on them?" Sam said.

Liam rattled off the list, and Bob stuck a pin in the map indicating each of the locations.

"Far from traffic," Sam reminded them.

"Okay, that narrows it down a touch, but not much," Liam said. "All of the locations are well-known tourist magnets, which means they're bound to be on the major routes, so traffic close by."

"Far from traffic," Sam repeated.

Liam nodded. "Let me get the details up for each of the locations."

He printed them off and distributed them around the team. Each member reported back with access from the car parks of each of the caves.

"I'm drawn to this one," Bob said.

He handed his sheet to Sam, and she read the information. "Has anyone ever been to Rydal Caves?"

"I have," Suzanna said, "It was years ago, on a school trip."

"It seems pretty popular on TripAdvisor," Liam announced.

"What can you tell us about the area, Suzanna? The tiniest detail will help us."

"Gosh, now you're testing me, boss. Can you give me a minute?"

"Of course. Liam, search the internet, see if there's a

larger map of the area."

"I was in the process of doing that, and I've found this."

Sam walked over to him and peered over his shoulder at the screen. "There's a twenty- to thirty-minute walk from the car park. Sounds feasible for him to put her there, however, I have one thing playing on my mind."

"Only the one?" Bob queried.

"How would he transfer the woman to the cave from the car, if it's a popular destination with the likelihood of hikers being around?"

"Maybe he took her up there in the dead of the night," Bob replied. "If he's local and knows the area well, maybe he's been out there, observing the place for a while, taking note of the footfall in the area and what times people go there. Is there a time limit on the car park?"

"Nope, there isn't You've raised some good points, Bob. Okay, I've heard enough. I'm willing to risk it and take a punt on that location. We'll all go, take two cars. Claire, you remain here, we'll keep you up to date on our progress."

"I was about to suggest the same. I don't think my back would be up to all that walking over rough terrain."

Sam smiled. "I'm wondering if mine will object, too. Come on, guys, let's get out there ASAP."

"It's going to take us at least an hour, just saying," Bob threw in for good measure.

"Overtime it is then, if that's what it takes to find this woman."

THEY ARRIVED at the car park just before seven. During the trip, Sam had rung home and explained the situation to Rhys. He'd told her not to worry and that he would take the dogs out for their evening walk. Bob had also called home and pissed Abigail off. They were due at a parents' evening at the school, and now she would be forced to attend alone. Bob was relieved but didn't relish the thought of going home if Abigail was going to be in one of her moods.

With torches and a couple of blankets to hand, the group set off at a fast pace that dwindled the closer they got to the cave.

"We'll stick together in there, don't take any unnecessary risks, you hear me?" Although her warning was to the group, Sam made a point of looking at Liam when she said it.

The team all agreed with either a nod or by raising their thumbs.

"Okay, buddy up with someone and remain with that person at all times. Shout if you find her. I doubt if our phones will get a reception in there. Any questions?"

The team shook their heads.

She could tell by the way they were all fidgeting that they were eager to get on with the search. "Let's go. Good luck. Work swiftly and efficiently. None of us know what the terrain is going to be like in there, so be vigilant. That's enough from me."

Fortunately, she'd had a pair of wellies in the boot of her car from walking the dogs around the lake at the weekend.

Sam and Bob led the way into the large mouth of the cave.

"Sophie, are you here?" Sam called.

The team stood still and listened. They were greeted by silence. Sam picked a path through the rocks, larger stones and the puddles of water at the mouth of the cave. Bob held a torch in front of him to guide them. The others spanned out, using their own torches. They checked everywhere, in all the nooks and crannies close to the entrance, but there was no sign of Sophie. They reached the inner part of the cave, where it began to narrow, and again Sam called out the woman's name only to be greeted with yet more silence.

She glanced at Bob, and he gave her a helpless look that matched the feeling running through her.

She has to be here, this can't be a waste of time. He wouldn't dare! How do I know that? I don't bloody know this tosser from Adam.

"We can't give up," she said. "I would never forgive myself if someone came out here tomorrow and found her... dead."

"I'm not suggesting we give up," Bob said. "We're going to need to search deeper, that's all. Maybe we should have contacted the search and rescue team before venturing up here by ourselves."

"It's far too late now. But yes, you're right, I should have thought about it and I neglected to." Sam inched further into the darkness, the damp seeping into her bones. "Sophie, if you can hear me but are unable to respond, can you throw something to make a noise?"

The group stood still and listened.

"I thought I heard something," Liam replied.

"What direction, Liam?"

"Way over to the right."

"Let's take a chance."

They headed towards the narrowing passage which seeped deeper into the cave. Sam picked up on a few choice words behind her when someone had slipped off a rock and into the pool of water she'd waded through in her wellies. She suspected that person was Alex, he was the type to think he could handle any given situation and fail.

"Sophie, we're coming. Can you give us another indication where you are? Throw something again."

This time Sam heard something hit the wall and drop into a pool of water. She upped her pace, and with the others close behind her, grappled her way through the confined space. A muffled cry alerted them over to the right of the passageway. The team all stopped and angled their torches to the area. There she was, with tape over her mouth, her hands tied in front of her and her legs bound with rope. Sam rushed to her side, and Oliver threw a foil blanket around Sophie's shoulders.

"It's okay. We've got you, you're safe now. This is going to hurt, brace yourself." Sam picked at the edge of the tape and ripped it from Sophie's mouth.

She cried out, and then the tears flowed.

Relief rippled through Sam. Granted, the young woman wasn't out of danger yet, she was half-naked and shivering, probably suffering from hypothermia, given the conditions she was found in with very little clothing to keep her warm. Sam couldn't help wondering how close to death the woman would have been if they hadn't taken the chance coming out to search for her. She shook her head, ridding herself of such thoughts. It was unnecessary to think that way, now that they had saved her.

"Are you able to stand?" Sam asked.

Sophie shook her head. "I don't think so. I can't even feel my legs, they're numb."

Liam stepped forward. "I can carry her back to the car."

Sam smiled and patted him on the shoulder. "You're my hero, Liam, bless you. Right, let's get her out of here. The light was fading when we arrived. It's going to be nearly dark out there now, which will only hamper our trek back to the car."

Liam smiled at Sophie. "Put your arms around my neck."

Oliver had already used his survival knife to cut through the ropes binding Sophie's limbs.

"I'm so grateful to you all for finding me. Does Ruby know?"

"She came to the station and reported you missing. I'll call her once we've got you tucked up in the car."

Liam hitched her slight body into his arms with ease. Sam

went ahead with Bob shining the torch ahead of her and Oliver guiding the way for Liam just behind them. The journey back seemed far shorter now that they had rescued Sophie. She was resting her head against Liam's chest, her eyelids drooping. The team covered her with the extra blankets they had with them, and the twenty-minute trek began in the near darkness.

Once they had reached the car, Liam eased Sophie into the back seat. She was trembling from head to toe.

"We're going to take her to the hospital," Sam said. "Thanks for all your help, guys. You head home. We'll catch up in the morning."

"Glad you're safe, Sophie," Suzanna called out, and the others followed suit by shouting something similar.

Sam threw Bob the keys to her car. "You drive, Bob, I'll sit in the back with Sophie. I want to call Ruby, too."

Once they were all settled and Bob was on the road, heading back towards Workington, Sam rang Ruby.

"Hi, Ruby. It's DI Sam Cobbs. Sorry to call so late. I have someone here who wants to speak with you." She handed the phone to Sophie.

"Hi, darling, it's me. They found me," Sophie said before she broke down in tears once more.

Ruby screamed on the other end. Sam smiled at the woman's obvious elation to have her wife back.

"How are you? Did they hurt you? Are you okay? Where are you?"

"I'm too tired to speak. I love you. I'll let the inspector answer all of your questions."

"Okay, silly me. I'm sorry. I'm overwhelmed that you're safe. I'll see you soon."

"Hi, Ruby, it's me again," Sam said, taking over the call. "We're on our way to Whitehaven Hospital. You can meet us there, if you like. We'll be about an hour."

"Shit! You're that far away? How? Why? Where was she found? I can't thank you enough for finding her. I'll shut up now."

Sam laughed. "It all turned out well in the end. She's fine, maybe suffering from a touch of hypothermia, hence the need for us to get her to hospital. We discovered her inside a cave. It really doesn't matter, we found her, that's all that counts."

"I'm so relieved. I'll see you at the hospital. Shall I go to the Accident and Emergency Department?"

"Yes, I'm going to call ahead, make sure she gets seen straight away. The queues have been horrendous there lately."

"Good idea. See you in about an hour, I'll get there early, though, I'm always early. I can't wait to hold her in my arms again. Drive safely."

"We will. You drive safely, too."

SAM HAD STUCK to her word and called ahead. Sophie was whisked through the A&E Department on a stretcher. The waiting area was heaving, Lord knew how long they would have waited if Sam hadn't contacted the hospital beforehand.

The wives' reunion was a tearful one which was to be expected. Sam and Bob both ended up misty eyed. The doctor checked Sophie over and reported his findings to Sam, Ruby and Bob who were all waiting in the family room.

"My, she has had a rough deal. I'm going to admit her overnight, just in case she has a relapse. The body is complex and sometimes catches us out when we least expect it. I would rather keep her here just to be on the safe side. As suspected, she is suffering from hypothermia, plus we're going to need to run further tests, make sure all her organs are performing how they should be. Stress can be detrimental to the way the system works at the best of times. Something like the ordeal she's been through will likely exacerbate things."

"We understand, Doctor," Sam said. "You know best. Is she up to seeing us?"

"Briefly, maybe you, Ruby. Any questions that need to be asked in order to further your investigation should be put on hold for now, Inspector. There's no denying the woman has been through a near-death experience, and her body and mind need to recover before she'll be able to function properly again."

"Okay, we'll leave it until the morning then. My main priority was finding her safe and well and getting her to the hospital to be treated. Everything else can wait for now."

"Good, very wise." The doctor nodded and faced Ruby. "Do you want to come with me?"

"Wild horses couldn't stop me," Ruby replied. She reached for Sam's hand and smiled. "I'm sorry you won't be able to see her tonight. Maybe it would be best if she slept and had time to recover."

"I understand completely. We'll drop by in the morning, I'll ring you first thing to make arrangements, if that's okay?"

"Thank you, you're very considerate."

"We need to go now," the doctor said impatiently.

Sam waved Ruby off and watched her and the doctor walk up the corridor together.

Bob heaved out a sigh beside her and said, "That was a close one."

"I'm glad we got to her when we did. I fear what might have happened to her had we been delayed."

"There's no doubt in my mind that she would have died. You saved the day, this time."

"*We* did. We all played our part in her rescue, even you."

"Bloody charming, that is. What now? Please tell me we're going to call it a day."

Sam glanced at her watch; it was gone midnight. "Damn, yes, let's go home. I'll drop you back at the station to collect your car. You'll have to send my apologies to Abigail. I'm sure she'll understand, in the circumstances."

"I hope so. With any luck she'll be asleep when I get in. If not, I think I'll be spending the night on the sofa."

"She wouldn't, would she?"

He raised an eyebrow. "You know what you women are like when you get a bee in your bonnet about something."

"Bloody hell. We're not all tarred with the same brush, you know. She's aware that you're doing overtime, isn't she?"

"Of course she is. Can we change the subject? I can feel myself getting worked up in a state inside."

Sam rubbed his arm. "I've got a spare room if you need one."

Bob's eyes lit up. "Don't tempt me."

"The offer is there, anytime you need it. Oops, maybe I should run that past Rhys first. No, I'm sure he'd agree to it."

"Thanks, I'm sure all will be good at home."

Sam dropped her partner back at the station car park and then drove home. She didn't call Rhys, thinking it was far too late to disturb him. Her heart skipped a beat when she rounded the corner and spotted a few of the lights on downstairs.

She parked the car and closed the door quietly, not wishing to wake any of the neighbours. Rhys was in the lounge, cuddling up to the two dogs. He was dozing and leapt to his feet as soon as she whispered hello.

"Oh God, I've been going out of my mind. Why didn't you ring me, let me know you were okay?"

They kissed, and she ran a hand over his face.

"I wasn't in any danger, I had my whole team there as backup. I'm sorry, it was gone twelve by the time I left the hospital. I thought about calling you but would have felt like shit if I'd disturbed your sleep."

"Hospital? What were you doing there?" He held her at arm's length, and his gaze roamed her body, looking for any sign of injury.

"No, it wasn't for me. We found the woman we were after and whisked her off to hospital to get checked over."

"Thank God. Where was she?"

"I could do with a drink and something to eat. I'll fix something and then fill you in."

"I made a casserole. I can heat it up in the microwave for you."

Her stomach rumbled at the thought of having a wholesome meal, but then she thought better of it at this time of night. "Maybe I'll settle for a sandwich instead, or some cheese on toast."

"I'll do it for you. Come through to the kitchen, you can tell me all about your adventure."

The dogs jumped off the sofa, still dopey from being woken by her arrival. Sam made a fuss of them and let them in the back garden to have a wee. She filled Rhys in while she watched them sniff around the garden and then start tugging at one of their toys which Sonny collected from the toy box under the lean-to.

"Jesus, she was lucky you found her when you did. What a callous bastard, to dump her where the likelihood she'd be found was minimal."

"I know. That was probably his intention. Maybe he wanted me to discover her still alive only for her to die once I'd found her."

"Blimey, if that's true, Sam, he's a very dangerous character indeed."

"Yep, someone we need to take off the streets as soon as we can. The one thing stopping us from doing that is the lack of evidence we have to hand. We haven't got a clue who he is. Maybe having a chat with Sophie in the morning will put a nail in his coffin."

Minutes later, Sam was tucking into a thick piece of crusty bread toasted with slices of cheese that Rhys had cooked in the air fryer for five minutes. He called the dogs in from the garden and got them settled in their baskets.

"This is delicious. I could eat this every night for a week and not get bored with it."

"It's a game changer, cooking it in the air fryer. So, how will your day pan out tomorrow? Or would you rather not discuss it?"

"I'm fine. I'll ring Ruby first thing, see how Sophie is, and then, if she's up to it, Bob and I will go back to the hospital to question her, see if she can point us in the right direction for tracking this bastard."

"Let's hope she gets through the night okay. Sorry, that came out wrong. I hope for your sake she isn't the type to want to block the whole episode from her mind. It wouldn't be the first time a victim has refused to revisit the trauma they went through."

"Gosh, don't say that. I'm sure that won't be the case. We'll find out soon enough." She emptied her glass of wine and swilled her plate under the hot tap. "If you don't mind, I'm going to see if I can get some sleep now. I'm going to need my wits about me in the morning."

"I was just about to suggest the same. You go up, I'll switch everything off and lock up down here."

Sam visited the bathroom and went through her nightly routine. Rhys went into the bathroom after her, and when he came out she was fast asleep, exhausted by her adventures.

CHAPTER 6

*D*espite dropping off to sleep as soon as her head hit the pillow, Sam woke up at three and tossed and turned the rest of the night, haunted by her dreams of not being able to save the first victim.

Rhys stretched beside her. "How are you?"

"Okay, I suppose. I need to find some form of relaxation to keep me asleep once I've dropped off. I've been awake since three."

He threw an arm over her and pulled her close. "I have a solution for your problem."

Sam kissed him and laughed. "Maybe we'll try it out later, but now I have to get up and start my day." She threw back the quilt and walked into the en suite.

"Spoilsport," he called after her.

She showered and held her face under the hot water for longer than normal, hoping to revive herself enough to get her brain functioning properly for what lay ahead. After drying herself, she picked out her best black suit and accompanied it with a white blouse then blow-dried her hair, thinking how long it had grown and that a trip to the hairdresser's was in order.

When she ventured downstairs, Rhys was fixing a fry-up for them both, the dogs at his feet, waiting for their crispy bit of bacon to be put in their dishes. She kissed him and slid her arms around his waist. He turned and embraced her in a lingering kiss.

"Good morning, beautiful, and how are you on this sunny day?"

"I'm fine, now I've had my shower. Not too much for me, I'm still full from what I ate last night, whatever that was."

"You can't be."

"Believe me, I am. Not everyone can stash food away like you can and not suffer from their gluttony."

"Bloody hell, that's a tad harsh. So what if I enjoy my food? Mum always used to tell me I had hollow legs growing up."

She chuckled. "Yeah, but it's when you're older you'll need to worry about it."

"I'll deal with that issue when old age hits me and not before."

He served up the breakfast. Hers was considerably smaller than his, thank goodness.

After devouring the greasy fry-up, Sam got both the dogs ready and walked them around the block while Rhys, at his insistence, cleaned up the kitchen. Then she dropped Sonny off next door to Doreen and headed into work.

When she arrived, the team were already at their desks. There was a buzz filling the room after last night's excitement and successful rescue.

"Morning, all. Everyone all right today?"

"They appear to be, boss," Bob replied. He left his chair and prepared Sam a mug of coffee which he deposited on her desk while she flicked through the mail.

She exhaled a relieved sigh. "No unexpected notes in that lot."

"Great news. What's first on the agenda today?"

"This lot can wait until later, I needed to be sure there wasn't another letter from him before we set off for the hospital."

"Ah, right. Have you checked in with Ruby yet?"

"I'm about to do that now. Once she gives us the go-ahead, we'll make a move."

"I've got Liam and Oliver looking into the CCTV footage around the post box and also the area of the car park, not that there is likely to be much out that way."

"It's a start. I agree, they're more likely to find something around the post box. Let's hope so anyway. Let me try and contact Ruby while I have my drink and take a cursory peek through the post, and then we'll shoot over to the hospital to see Sophie."

"I'll leave you to it."

Bob left the room, and she fished out her mobile from her coat pocket and dialled Ruby's number. "Hi, Ruby. It's DI Sam Cobbs. How are things this morning?"

"Oh, hi, Inspector. I've not long rung the hospital to check on Sophie. She's had a fitful night, apparently. The nurses felt it was better to give her something to help her sleep. She settled down afterwards. They've told me to leave it until ten before I visit her."

"Fair enough. What if my partner and I come to the hospital at around ten-thirty?"

"Sounds good to me. Sorry to put you out like this."

"You're not, so there's no need to apologise. I'll see you later. Take care."

Sam sank into her chair and busied herself with her least-liked chore. Her mind wandered back to the case now and again, but in the main, she was able to sift through her emails and letters with ease, for a change.

Bob checked in on her ten minutes after she had begun her mission and had topped up her caffeine levels with another mug of coffee.

"Have the boys stumbled across anything yet, or am I asking too much, too soon?" she asked.

Bob laughed. "The latter. It's far too soon to come up with a result on that front, you know how things pan out."

"Worth asking, though, eh? We'll leave at ten, all right?"

"Fine by me."

SAM PARKED the car in a spot as close as she could get to the hospital entrance and put the sign on the dashboard, 'police officer on duty'. Sometimes it worked, depending on whether the car park attendant was in a generous mood or not.

She asked at reception which ward Sophie had been taken to, something she'd neglected to ask Ruby on the phone earlier. The receptionist gave them directions to the Women's Ward which was on the second level.

Sam smiled at the nurse and showed her ID. "Hi, we're here to have a chat with Sophie Meskill. I checked with Ruby earlier and arranged to come at ten-thirty."

"Ruby did mention you were on your way. Sophie is a little groggy this morning, so please, be gentle with her."

"Of course, that goes without saying."

"The bed with the curtains drawn." The nurse pointed down the ward at the last bed on the left.

"Thanks. We should be out of your hair soon."

"No problem. Hope all goes well, that woman has been through a terrible ordeal."

Sam nodded and walked ahead of Bob down the ward.

Feeling awkward, Sam poked her head around the curtain. "Hi, Ruby, Sophie. Is it all right to come in?"

"Please do. I'll see if I can grab another chair," Ruby said. "Here, take mine for now."

"No, sit there. Bob can source another one, I'll sit over here."

Bob left and returned a few moments later. He placed his chair on the other side of the bed, next to Sam's. "How are you this morning, Sophie?"

"Honestly?"

Sam nodded.

"Everything is a bit of a blur. I was restless last night, so they knocked me out, and it has left me with a very thick head. You'll have to forgive me if I'm not at my best."

"Don't worry. I'm not going to push you, however, we're going to need to know a little about what you went through. I didn't want to bombard you with questions in the car on the journey here last night."

"Thank you. I think I was in shock." She shuddered and clasped her arms around her body.

Ruby dipped into the bedside cupboard. She removed a cardigan and placed it around Sophie's shoulders. "We'll soon get you warmed up."

"Thanks, love."

Sam could see the love in both women's eyes, and it gladdened her heart that the outcome, on this occasion, had been a good one, unlike the first victim.

"In your own time, can you go over what happened?"

"I'll try. I don't think I'll be good on times and the finer details, so you'll need to forgive me for that."

"Just tell us what you can remember. There's no pressure to get all the facts right at this stage, we can revisit anything we need to at a later date."

"Okay. I was at the gym. I said goodbye to my friends

and split from them. They were parked up the road, but I chose to park in the gym's car park. Thinking about it, maybe I should have left the car under a streetlight instead; it was fairly dark where I left it. That was the first mistake I made that evening. The man was waiting for me. He pounced and knocked me out. He shoved me in the boot of his car. When I woke up, he forced me out of the vehicle and took me inside a small cottage. It was pretty remote. He tied my hands together but left my feet undone. He went out to the car, and not being the type of person to just sit around and wait for things to happen, I took the opportunity which opened up for me to escape. I fooled him for a few minutes, but he doubled back, caught me getting in his car. I took off. It wasn't easy driving with my hands tied, but what was the alternative? Stay there, allow him to..." Her head dipped, and she mumbled, "To rape me again. I couldn't, it was a case of fight or flight, and I chose to run."

Tears dropped onto her cheek, and Ruby dutifully wiped them away.

"It's okay. Take your time," Sam said.

"No, I want to tell you. If I get it out into the open maybe it will help me heal quicker. Isn't that what the therapists encourage you to do?"

"That's right. But after a while, not directly after an incident like this has occurred. So, no pressure from me."

"I was lying here last night, and every time I closed my eyes I saw his face, sneering at me, getting closer... I couldn't get away from it and cried out. I feel bad about waking the other patients on the ward, but it was like he was still here, taunting me, getting ready to pounce on me again."

"It's okay, you're safe now," Ruby said, gently rubbing the back of Sophie's hand.

"I'm so relieved to be away from him."

Sam left it a few seconds and then asked, "What happened when you drove off?"

"Sorry, yes, he must have known where I would go. He cut me off, jumped out of the trees. I was distracted, scared and, well, I drove into a tree." She touched the lump on her forehead. "I got knocked out. When I woke up, he'd tied me to the bed, back at the cottage." She paused, and her breathing became erratic, her chest rising and falling faster and faster.

Sam placed her hand on Sophie's arm. "We can stop there, if it's getting too much for you."

Sophie shook her head. "No, I want to go on. Just give me a moment to get my emotions under control."

"Take all the time you need."

Ruby rose from her seat and planted a kiss on Sophie's cheek and wiped away her tears. "There's no rush, in your own time, darling."

Sophie's head tipped back against the pillow, and she sucked in a large breath. "I'm fine."

Sam noticed Sophie's breathing had returned to near normal and knew she was going to be all right. "Can you recall what type of car he had?"

"I'm hopeless when it comes to cars, Ruby will tell you that."

"I can confirm," Ruby said, grinning.

"But after the crash, he had another car. No idea where he got it from. I don't know if he had a spare stashed in the garage or what? Or even if there was a garage at the cottage, that I can't remember, sorry."

"No problem. We'll see if anyone has reported a car being stolen yesterday and go from there. How did he react to you attempting to escape? Or is that a daft question?"

"He punished me. Stripped most of my clothes off and kept me tied to the bed." Again, her chin sank to her chest, and she sighed. "And took advantage of me… numerous times. How could he do that? I told him I was gay, that's why I think he punished me in that way."

Ruby stared at Sam and shook her head. "That's a crime in itself, taking someone against their will, especially when they're from the LGBT community, isn't it? What a despicable scrote he is. He needs to be caught, and quickly, before he can do this to someone else. His type always do, don't they? He won't stop with Sophie, will he?"

"I think you're right, which is why I felt it was important to come here this morning to speak with you, Sophie. Would you be able to give us a description of this man? I know the last thing you want to do is conjure up his image in your mind, but knowing if he has any specific features, like scars or anything along those lines, will go a long way to helping us find him."

Sophie's eyes widened. "Yes, he had a scar on his forehead, above his right eye."

"A deep scar? Can you tell me how long it was?"

"It went from above his eye into his hairline, so pretty long, maybe three inches."

"That's brilliant. What colour hair did he have?"

"Dark brown, almost black, I suppose. It was short, just over his collar, and he had brown eyes. His nose was a little twisted, possibly been broken in the past, but I noticed there was a cut on it, too. Ah, yes, he also had a swelling under one eye, and it was slightly discoloured."

"Like a black eye? Maybe his nose was broken recently and that was the result, a black eye. This is so good, Sophie, you're amazing to be able to recall all of these details, in the circumstances."

"I'm determined to help you find him. There's no way he should be allowed to do this to another woman." She swallowed and then whispered, "I got the impression that he was going to kill me. Maybe that's why he dumped me at the cave." She shuddered again.

"I don't suppose you saw how long it took you to drive to the cave from the cottage?"

"It was around forty minutes. I took note of the clock on the dashboard."

"How did he get you to the cave?"

"I walked most of the way. He dressed me in some of his gear, told me that mine stank of sweat. Not surprising, I had worked out in it on Tuesday. I had intended to go straight home to have a shower and get changed, I always do. Then, before he left me in the cave, he stripped me. I pleaded with him not to leave me there, fearing I was going to die from the cold. He simply laughed in my face and told me if I died it was only what I deserved."

"Cold-hearted fucking sod," Ruby muttered. She gathered Sophie's hand in her own. "I hope the inspector and her team can track him down from what you've told her. I can see how tired you are, love, I think we should call it a day now."

Sam nodded. "That's fine with me. You've got my number, should Sophie think of anything else. I can't thank you enough for speaking with us so soon after the appalling incident. I'm so glad you're safe."

Sophie released her hand from Ruby's and clutched at Sam's arm. "Please get him. He's a sex pest, doesn't care who he hurts. Wait, there's one more thing, I didn't ask him but I remember him from being at the gym, I'm not sure if he was there as someone's guest or whether he's an actual member of the gym himself."

"That's great. We can delve into it once we leave here. You rest now, you've amazed all of us with your determination. Seek help from a counsellor if you need it, Sophie, don't be too proud to ask, will you?"

"I won't. I think Ruby and I will get through this together.

She's my rock. Our love is solid, despite what the universe has thrown at us over the past few days."

"That's right. There's no way what this moron has done will ever damage our relationship, we refuse to let that happen. We'll move on and be happier than we were before, if that's at all possible, just to spite the bastard."

Sam smiled. "That's the spirit, ladies. Ring me if you need any advice or aren't sure about anything. I'll always be there for you."

"Thank you, from both of us," Sophie said. "And I wanted to say thank you personally to you and your team for pulling out all the stops, working long after your shift had ended yesterday, just to save me."

"It's all in a day's work. Take care, both of you."

Sam and Bob rose from their seats, and Bob removed the spare chair from the area.

"We'll be in touch if Sophie remembers anything of note," Ruby replied. "Thank you, Inspector, for everything."

Sam's heart lifted, and she joined Bob at the reception desk.

"Everything go all right? The doctor is bound to ask when he conducts his rounds," the nurse asked.

"She did really well. We came away before she got too tired. She's a very brave lady. Take care of her for us."

"Don't worry, we will. I'll make sure she gets an extra portion of jelly for afters, how's that?"

Sam giggled. "I'm sure she'll be very impressed, hard not to be. Thanks for letting me see her."

"You're welcome."

They left the hospital. Sam looked at the grey sky and gulped down a few lungfuls of fresh air.

"Where to now?"

"We need to pay the gym a visit."

"I thought you might say that."

. . .

THEY ARRIVED at the gym around fifteen minutes later. The car park was heaving.

"Busy place, I didn't even know it existed, did you?" Sam said.

"I've been here as a friend's guest once or twice."

Sam got out of the car and surveyed the area. "The section in the middle there doesn't have any form of lighting."

"I bet that's where she parked then. Why don't women consider the safety aspect of where they park their cars nowadays? It's the first thing I tell Abigail, if she goes out at night, to make sure she parks where it is well lit. It's a deterrent, if nothing else."

"You're going to hate me... I must admit, up until now, I've never considered it. In my defence, before you leap down my throat, I shouldn't have to. Is it something men should consider as well? No, well then, where's the equality in that?"

"Don't get me started. It's about practicability and common sense, isn't it?"

"If you say so."

"I do. Everyone needs to consider their safety these days, the statistics will back me up on that. It's not just women who get jumped on the way to their cars at night. Therefore, everyone needs to take care in my opinion."

"I promise to bear it in mind in the future, okay?"

"Do what you want with the advice, you of all people shouldn't have needed telling anyway. Not in your position."

"In my position? You think I'm a prime target for someone jumping out on me when I'm least expecting it, is that what you're saying?"

He shrugged and walked towards the entrance of the gym, leaving Sam staring after him, open-mouthed.

Bob was standing in the reception area when she caught up with him. He took a step back and gestured for her to go ahead of him.

Sam approached the receptionist and produced her warrant card. "DI Sam Cobbs, and this is my partner, DS Bob Jones. Is the manager around?"

"Terry is with a client at the moment. Can I help?"

"It's regarding an incident that happened in your grounds on Tuesday, involving one of your members."

"Oh, I see." She peered over her shoulder through the glass screen at the gym below. "He shouldn't be too long. I think he's finishing off the session with Mrs Rogers now. It's probably better if you speak with him. I'll nip down there and let him know you're here. Take a seat. I'll be right back."

"Thanks. We'll grab a coffee from the machine, if that's okay?"

She opened the top drawer of her desk and removed a couple of tokens. "Here you go, on me."

Sam smiled. "You're too kind, thanks."

The young brunette, dressed in a velour leisure suit, jumped out of her seat and trotted through the reception area and entered the gym.

Sam gave the tokens to Bob. "Make yourself useful and get the drinks." She moved closer to the glass partition and watched the receptionist skip through the gym and speak to a muscle-bound giant of a man. He turned to look up at Sam, and she smiled and waved to him. He gave her the thumbs-up and then raised three fingers.

Bob nudged her elbow and offered her a plastic cup that was hot to touch.

"Jesus, these cups should be against the bloody law, they could cause some serious damage, in the wrong hands."

Bob rolled his eyes. "Whatever. Is that him?"

"I'm presuming so. Three minutes, he said."

"You can read his lips from that distance? You never cease to amaze me."

Sam didn't bother correcting him. She sat in one of the comfy low-level seats and read the noticeboard to the side of her. "How long has it been since you were last here?"

"A couple of years, why?"

"Is it the same owner or manager?"

"How the heck should I know? I used the equipment and was out of here at the end of the session. I'm never one to hang around, mingling with people I don't know. Can't abide that."

"You're a miserable sod at the best of times, Bob. How you've got any friends at all is beyond me."

"Says you. When was the last time you went out with any of your friends?"

"Don't go there. We lead busy lives, and it's hard to find the time to catch up."

"There you go then, don't fling shit at me, not when you're in the same bloody boat."

"Okay, I'll give you that one. Have your drink, be careful you don't burn that sharp tongue of yours."

"I won't. Thanks for the warning."

They sat in silence until Terry appeared in front of them.

"You wanted to see me?"

"If you have the time." Sam struggled to get to her feet, what with the seat being so low.

Terry offered to lend a hand and yanked on her arm. The movement was carried out with a superhuman force that caused her chest to flatten against his steel-like pecs.

Sam blushed and stared up at him. "Pleased to meet you."

He grinned, displaying perfect white teeth that gleamed against his fake tan, or maybe he had picked it up on an early trip abroad to a sunnier climate. "The pleasure was all mine," he assured her. He intentionally pumped his pecs wildly against her breasts.

Embarrassed by the man's muscles playing havoc against her upper torso, Sam took a step back and almost toppled into the chair again. Bob tutted to her left. She ignored him and brushed herself down.

Quickly recovering her composure, she said, "Thanks for taking the time out to speak with us. Do you have an office?"

"Doesn't every manager? I can spare you ten minutes. In that time I have to grab a quick bite to eat. Cheryl, can you fix me a shake and get me some protein bars from the storeroom? I don't have time to get to the shop and back and finish the meeting with these officers before Mrs Wilkinson arrives."

"Consider it done. I'll bring them through, Terry."

"You've got drinks, so that's you sorted. Walk this way." His strides were long and resolute.

Sam had trouble keeping up with his pace. Bob didn't, and he glanced over his shoulder and pulled a face at her. She discreetly ran a finger up either side of her nose, forming a V-sign. Her partner laughed and entered the office behind the great hulk who went by the name of Terry.

"Take a seat. Make it snappy. Like I've already told you, I have a schedule to stick to, I'm the utter professional. I've never let a client down yet, and I don't intend to start now either."

"We promise not to take up too much of your time. It's about what happened in your car park on Tuesday. You are aware of the incident, aren't you?"

"No. Correction, I'm aware of what I was told occurred, I've yet to see the evidence that something actually went down."

"Ruby Meskill came to the gym to speak with you, didn't she?"

"No. What she did was come into the reception area screaming the odds at me from a distance. I don't entertain people who haven't got a civil tongue in their heads."

"What? Did you even consider how fraught and upset she might have been, knowing that her wife was missing?"

His boulder-sized shoulders rose and fell again. "Not my problem. My job is to ensure my clients get fit. I told her she needed to take a trip down to the nearest cop shop to file a missing person report, and she flew at me, fists pounding at my chest, and then her claws came out and scratched my neck. Thank fuck she wasn't six inches taller, she might have done some serious damage to my best feature." He placed his hands on either side of his sun-kissed face and then extended his neck to show off the temporary disfigurement Ruby had left him with.

"I'm sorry she resorted to attacking you. All I can say in her defence is that she was going out of her mind with worry, as would ninety percent of the population, I suspect."

"Like I said, not my problem, she was bang out of order. She's lucky I didn't ring you lot and lay an assault charge at her door as well."

"I'm glad you didn't. Anyway, it has since come to our attention that her wife, Sophie, had been abducted and was held by a man who kidnapped her while she was on the way to her car, which was parked on your premises."

Clearly irate, he bounced upright in his chair. "Are you having a laugh?"

"Nope, I'm not one to make light of situations like this, Terry. Sophie Meskill's life was in imminent danger, that's why Ruby was doing her utmost to find her wife. A little consideration and understanding in the circumstances wouldn't have gone amiss."

"Now wait just a minute, she didn't tell me that. My

assumption was that they'd had a blazing row and her wife had stormed off and just left her car here."

"To be fair, Ruby wasn't aware until yesterday what had happened to her wife, not fully."

He shrugged. "Shit happens, but scratching the hell out of someone whom you're seeking help from isn't the answer, is it?"

"You're right, it isn't. Can we move on from this issue, as we're restricted for time?"

"Okay. What do you need to know?"

"When Sophie was rescued, we interviewed her, and she told us that she recognised the man from when she had attended the gym."

"What? He comes here?"

"So it would seem, yes."

"Bugger. What's his name? I'll kick him out and refuse him access to our facilities in the future."

"That's just it, we've got nothing more than that. We're not aware of his name or the make of the car he bundled Sophie into. That's where you come in. We wondered if you have any cameras on site. If so, maybe we could have a look through them, try to ascertain who this man is."

He sighed and glanced at his watch. "Let me see what I can get organised." He marched out of the office and returned a few moments later. "Les is going to fill in for me with the client, tell her I've had a family emergency I need to attend to. Right, come with me, I'll show you our security system. I have to warn you, it's pretty limited. I've never felt the need to have a hi-tech system in place."

He walked ahead of them, and Bob rolled his eyes at Sam.

"Or the need to make sure all areas of the car park are well lit at all times," he muttered, sounding pissed off.

"We'll tackle that issue afterwards."

"Don't worry, I have no intention of letting it drop."

They followed him back through the reception area and entered a small room on the other side.

"I know, you can barely swing a cat in here. It does the job. Tuesday you said, right?"

"Correct. Sorry, Sophie was too shaken up by her ordeal to give us the exact time."

"Do you know at what time her gym session was?"

"No, possibly early evening. Can you check from around five-thirty?"

He flicked through the disc cases on the shelf above his head and removed one of the discs which he inserted into the machine. The screen split into sections, four images in all.

"This is great," Sam said. "So you have the reception area and car park covered at the same time. That'll save us trawling through different discs."

"Yeah, that's the way I wanted it set up when the guys installed the system."

"Do you know Sophie Meskill?" Sam asked.

"Not personally. She's never had a one-to-one session with me."

"How many members do you have?"

"Over three thousand in total. Granted, there are quite a few who have let their membership lapse. I suppose we have around a third to a half of that total who use the gym regularly, at least once a month. The figures always rise in January, you know, people having good intentions to begin the new year."

"I'm one of those people. My sister bought me a gym membership as a birthday gift a few years ago. I attended the first session, then life got in the way and I never got around to using it again. It wasn't here, though. Your facilities seem pretty good."

"Thanks. Our equipment is all top notch. Either people take to lifting weights or they don't. That's why we put on different classes, such as aerobics for those who still want to get fit without building muscle mass."

"Makes sense to offer an alternative." Sam continued asking questions while her focus remained on the screen. "How many cameras do you have, covering the car park?"

"One at the main entrance and another towards the rear."

"We've seen the area where Sophie's car was parked, and I don't think that spot was covered. Might be an idea to up the cameras you have out there in the near future."

"This is the only incident of this nature we've had since we opened. I'm not sure the extra expense would be warranted."

Sam cocked an eyebrow and glanced at him. "Sophie was abducted. If we hadn't rescued her, she would have been killed by this man."

"I repeat, it's an isolated incident. I'm sorry she went through such a horrendous ordeal, but cameras cost money, and I don't think it would be worth the extra investment."

"What about getting extra lights installed out there? Some areas are darker than others, inviting dubious characters in our society to leap at the chance to do something bad," Bob said.

Sam could tell his anger was mounting. She shot him a warning glance, telling him to back off.

"I'll get it sorted as and when time permits. As I keep saying, this was a one-off incident."

"Which could multiply with the snap of my fingers," Sam added before Bob had a chance to jump in with one of his notoriously sarcastic comments.

"Wait, isn't that her?" Bob pointed at the screen.

Sam took a step nearer for a closer look as the images were slightly grainy, as usual with these things. "I think it is. Yes, here she is with her friends. They should say goodbye and go their separate ways soon."

As if on cue, Sophie went towards the car park, and her friends set off in the opposite direction.

"And that's as much as we're going to get because the damn camera coverage doesn't stretch to her car." Bob slammed his fist against his thigh.

"All right, man, it is what it is, there's no point you getting all hot-headed about this. I'll sort it."

Bob eyed Terry with disdain. "Really? What will it take for you to fulfil that promise? For someone to lose their life?"

"It won't come to that, but I'll tell you this, standing here, trying to bully me into action isn't going to help. I'm the type who prefers to dig their heels in when ordered to do something, as far as my business is concerned. So back off, chum."

Sam cringed and immediately took her hands out of her jacket pockets, ready to restrain her partner, aware how irate he was becoming, the more time he spent in this jerk's presence.

"I repeat, your security is an issue for your customers," Bob said. "One woman has already been kidnapped. Who's to say this maniac hasn't chosen your car park as his hunting ground to kidnap yet more women because you couldn't be arsed to fork out for more cameras?"

"Sergeant Jones, that's enough. The point has been raised and responded to several times, we need to move on," Sam interjected.

"Yeah, listen to your boss, she seems a wise bird to me."

Terry's condescending tone and words put Sam's teeth on edge. She pulled in a couple of calming breaths and turned her attention back to the screen once more. "She went out of sight here. Can we stick with it, watch the exit to the car park, see what cars leave the area within the next five minutes or so?"

"I can switch up the cameras, get that one on full screen, if it will help," Terry replied.

"That would be great."

Terry pressed a few buttons, and the image was enhanced and far easier to see. Three minutes later, and they saw a dark vehicle leaving the car park, but the number plate had been obscured with mud, Sam assumed intentionally.

"Bugger, should have known that would be the case. Never mind, we've tried our best. Is there any chance we can grab a copy of Sophie leaving the gym with her friends and the car exiting?"

"I can do that now for you."

Despondency overwhelmed Sam. She had set her heart on going to the gym to seek the answers they needed to get the investigation rolling. She saw this as a major set-back that she struggled to believe would be easily overcome.

Terry handed Sam the copy of the disc and saw them back to the main entrance. "Sorry the news wasn't better," he said sheepishly.

"It's fine. We believe the kidnapper is keen on playing games with us. Maybe he chose the location intentionally. As my partner suggested, it might be a good idea to make a few changes to your security in the near future."

"I will, I promise."

Sam and Bob left the gym and returned to the car.

"That wasn't helpful," Sam said.

"What wasn't?" Bob asked.

"You, spitting your dummy out back there."

"I didn't. All I did was point out the obvious. You'll thank me if it saves another woman from getting kidnapped."

"He's promised to make the changes. Whether he will or not remains to be seen."

"Maybe we should call back in a couple of months and check."

"Hopefully it won't be necessary. I think we should drop by the lab on our way back to the station, see if they can enhance the image of the car, maybe get a sneaky peek at the kidnapper."

"Yeah, right, I wouldn't bank on it if I were you."

Des was coming out of one of the side rooms when they arrived in the reception area. "And to what do we owe the pleasure?" he asked. His gaze dropped to the disc case Sam was holding. "Ah, more evidence you need us to take a look at, eh?"

"If you have the time. We believe we've got the killer/kidnapper's car on the disc. We need you guys to enhance it for us."

"Kidnapper? Am I missing something?"

"We could discuss it over a coffee in your office."

"Or you could let me get on with my work and stop wasting my time and tell me right here and now," Des fired back.

"Shit! Okay. My team and I worked long into the night last night to rescue the killer's latest victim."

He gasped and frowned.

"You weren't needed to attend the scene because we found her safe and well. She's in hospital after her ordeal. She was kidnapped outside the gym she had attended and held in a cottage for a few days by the killer. Yes, he violated her numerous times before he left her, half-naked, in a cave."

"Bloody hell. May I ask how you found her?"

"The killer led us on a treasure hunt. He's toying with us."

"Shit! Hate these types of cases, it heaps added pressure on the SIO, and that's where slip-ups are made."

"You what? Not this SIO. We swiftly solved the riddle he sent us and managed to rescue the woman before she succumbed too heavily to the elements."

"She had hypothermia, I take it?"

"That's right. Anyway, we've retraced her steps and came up trumps with the car, or so we believe. If you can get your guys to make it a priority, I'd appreciate it."

"What's it worth?"

Sam heaved out a sigh. "Me being nice to you for a change, how's that?"

He laughed. "I'll take that."

"While we're here, can we chase up the other evidence we dropped in a few days ago, the letters I received?"

"Feel free. I've got a PM to carry out. I'll be in touch soon. Glad you have one less victim heading my way. Keep vigilant. By the sounds of it, this killer has every intention of running you ragged."

"I kind of came to that conclusion all by myself."

Des waved and sped off down the corridor, leaving Sam and Bob to hunt around for the right person who was carrying out the tests on the notes. Dave assured her that he was just about to contact Sam with the results.

"I've saved you the bother. What have you found, if anything?"

He shrugged and shook his head. "That's just it, there was nothing on there. Correction, I picked up a few prints only on one and when I ran them through the system I found that they belonged to you and the desk sergeant at the station, that's about it."

"Crap, I'd been expecting that to be honest. We've got a devious killer on our hands who appears to know every trick in the book."

"Let's hope he doesn't lead you a merry dance."

"I fear it's too late for that. Thanks anyway. I doubt if I've heard the last of him. I'll send over any future notes I receive, just in case he manages to slip up."

"Do that. I'll be sure to get to work on them ASAP."

Sam and Bob left the lab and headed back to the station.

"Where do we go from here?" Bob asked once they were belted into the car.

"We keep digging with the CCTV footage and hope that we come up with something soon."

"Liam and Oliver are doing their best, but with limited footage to go on, it's a near impossible task for them. What about the members at the gym?"

Sam feared what Bob was about to suggest. "Go on, what about them?"

"Should we go through them? Run them through the system?"

"Three thousand of them? And in any case, running them through the system would only pick up on those with former criminal records. I shouldn't need to point that fact out to you, partner."

Out of her peripheral vision she saw his head wobble as he mimicked what she said. She punched him in the thigh.

"What was that for? I could have you up for assault."

"As if. Stop taking the piss out of me when you know I'm right."

"I'm not. I would never dream of doing that. Okay, so what's the answer, Sherlock?"

"Christ, how insulting of you to change my gender like that. Sherlock was a *male* fictional detective, in case you hadn't realised."

"Will there ever be a day where you won't feel the need to correct me?"

"The ball is in your court there, Bob. You keep showing your ignorance about certain facts and I'll keep pointing out the errors of your ways. Hey, you're lucky you have me as a partner who can brush these things off."

"I am? I'm so relieved," he said, his sarcasm emerging once more.

"Anyway, this investigation needs to take another direction soon or I fear we're going to get frustrated with it very quickly."

"The team are doing their darndest with the evidence we've supplied them with. Not sure what else we can do to get things going again, until the perp gets back in touch."

"The only time he's going to do that is if he either abducts or kills someone else." Sam slammed the heel of her hand onto the steering wheel.

"Hey, losing your cool about it isn't going to make a difference either."

"I know but it made me feel better, if only for a brief second or two."

"How's the hand by the way?"

She faced him and snarled, "It hurts. I'll get over it."

"Foolish behaviour always comes attached to painful consequences."

"Get you!"

CHAPTER 7

*G*arner followed Sam to the gym then to the lab but veered off in a different direction when it was obvious that she and her partner were heading back to the station. Elation filled him when he saw the frustration wrinkling her brows after she left the gym. They were even deeper when she exited the lab, which made his day.

The lights turned red. He rubbed his hands and glanced sideways at the pad sitting beside him on the passenger seat. He'd managed to do a lot of planning, whiling away the time during Sam's visits.

Plotting, always plotting. Either that or he would be scribbling down riddles with a specific aim in mind, to send to her, when the time was right, but first, he had yet another victim to source. He was on his way back to his cottage, aware that it would be silly for him to strike in broad daylight.

No, I'll wait until this evening. I've always liked dusk, under the glow of a glorious sunset the weathermen were predicting for this evening. Yes, I'll make my move then. But who? What shall I choose this time, young or old?

His groin twitched, and he laughed. "Young it is then."

The lights changed colour, and he put his foot down. He drove past a group of teenage girls on their way into town and smirked. "Oh yes, definitely young. I have an itch that needs scratching."

A FEW HOURS LATER, he emerged from the cottage appropriately dressed for the adventure that lay ahead of him.

He went on the prowl, driving past several pubs only to feel dejected when nothing came his way in the first hour or so. Then he changed his hunting ground and, finally, he struck gold when he spotted a woman waving farewell to her friends and going in the opposite direction to them.

Why do women do that? Why don't they stick together? Especially when there are evil shits like me around.

He chortled and dropped back, not wishing to alert her of his presence. Glancing up ahead, he tried to gauge which direction she was going to take. There were two possible ways, from what he could tell.

His adrenaline pumped at the prospect of capturing another victim. He checked the street, couldn't see anyone lingering anywhere. The time was right to make a move. He drove up behind her, but she changed direction at the last minute.

Has she spotted me? Have I slipped up and missed the chance?

He decided to go after her on foot and parked in the next space he found. After collecting the gaffer tape and knife from the passenger seat, he left the car, didn't bother locking it, and set off after her. Her pace was quick. She appeared to be using some form of headphones, listening to music or learning a language perhaps? It didn't matter, it was the distraction he needed to jump her. Keeping to the shadows, in case she turned around, he crept up behind her and slapped a hand over her mouth. She immediately struck out, hands and legs flying at him, catching him in the face and the shins at the same time. His temper surged, and he belted her across the face. Her head snapped to the right with force. She slipped to the ground, semi-conscious. He tore off a piece of tape and stretched it over her mouth, noting the colour and shape of her lips. His groin throbbed. Then he bound her hands with a plastic tie.

"What the fuck are you doing?" A man came out of the house closest to them.

Shit, I've messed up. "She's my girlfriend, we're fooling around, it's a game we like to play. You know, a sex game."

The man stared at him and shook his head. "Don't give me that bullshit." He held up his phone and prodded at it. "Yes, police. I need their assistance at my house. I've got a man here, he's trying to abduct a woman. Please hurry. Yes, the address is Humberside Road, Workington. Number thirty-nine."

Garner entered panic mode, knowing the police would be there soon. The woman was dazed at his feet. He left her and turned his attention to the man. He ran at him, catching him off-guard enough that he dropped the phone. Garner stamped on it and grabbed the man around the throat. "See yourself as some kind of hero, do you? I'm going to give you a good hiding, that'll teach you to think twice before interfering in what doesn't concern you in the future." He punched him several times.

Despite the man's size, he turned out to be a coward, all mouth and no action. The more times he struck the man, the more pumped Garner felt, revelling in the violence. He removed the knife from his jacket and stabbed the man in the chest.

Out of the corner of his eye, he saw the woman get to her

feet. He left the man lying on his path and pounced on the woman who was about to take off.

"Oh no you don't, you're coming with me." He pointed at the blood pouring out of the man and sneered, "Try anything rash, and you'll end up like him, dead. Got that?"

Tears mixed with snot, and she nodded, her gaze shooting between the wannabe hero and Garner. She mumbled something, but the tape suppressed her words. He'd heard enough. The police were on their way, and he needed to get the woman out of there before they showed up. In the distance, he could hear the wail of a siren getting closer.

"Come with me. Struggle, and I'll end your life here and now," he warned again, in case she hadn't received the message the first time.

She nodded, and more tears seeped onto her cheeks. He gripped her arm and steered her towards the car, upping his pace as the wail got louder.

Shit, they're only streets away now. I'm going to get caught.

He managed to get the woman tucked into the footwell of the passenger seat and slip behind the steering wheel just as a patrol car showed up. Nerves jangling, he started the car and casually drove past the police car. Two coppers had rushed out of the vehicle to assist the man he'd attacked. *Is he dead or alive?* He hated leaving loose ends.

The woman sobbed. She tried to speak, but it was useless, he couldn't understand what she was saying.

He patted the seat beside him and put the child lock on the doors at the same time. "You can sit up here now, the choice is yours."

She hesitated for a few seconds and then chose to stay where she was.

"Whatever. Stay down there, you miserable bitch, see if I care."

She whimpered and covered her face with her bound hands.

He drove the couple of miles to his cottage, laughing.

CHAPTER 8

Sam hadn't been at home long when the call came in. The last thing she'd told the night desk sergeant was to ring her if news of any abductions or murders were received during his shift. And now, here he was, calling her to break the news she'd been dreading to hear.

"Sorry to disturb you, ma'am. It would appear that you tempted fate before you left."

"Okay, Sergeant, tell me what we've got." She held up Rhys's hand and kissed the back of it, apologising for what was about to happen. She suspected she would soon be needed to attend a bad crime scene.

"A possible abduction of a female. A man came out of his house, saw a man attacking a woman. He gave a cock-and-bull story about them playing some kind of sex game and then he attacked the man. Stabbed him in the chest. Fortunately, he missed his heart by half an inch."

"Shit. All right, is he up to speaking with me?"

"I'm sure he will be, ma'am. He called the police while the suspect was there, before he got stabbed, so our guys were already on the way to him before the man tried to finish him off."

"And the woman?"

"No sign of her when my lads arrived."

Sam blew out a breath and cursed. "Not good. Any other witnesses?"

"I went ahead and got my guys to start the house-to-house enquiries. None of them have reported in so far. I'll chase it up now, if you like?"

"If you wouldn't mind. What's the man's name, and I'll pay him a visit?"

"Steve Palmer. He's at Whitehaven. Odds are that he'll be moved to either Carlisle or Newcastle soon, depending on the extent of his injuries."

"I'll get over there now. Thanks, Sergeant. Let me know if anything else comes to light this evening."

"I will. Drive safely, ma'am."

Sam ended the call and jumped to her feet. "Sorry to run out on you like this, it would appear the 'Changer of Lives' has struck again. I've got an injured witness I need to question at the hospital."

"Do you want me to come with you?"

"That's very sweet of you, but no, you stay here and keep the dogs company. There's no telling how long I'm likely to be."

His smile failed to reach his eyes.

She touched a hand to his face and then kissed him. "Thanks for caring."

"Always. Ring me, let me know what's going on when you can."

"I will. Hey, I should be back within an hour or two, that's the plan, fingers crossed."

They shared another brief kiss. Sam ruffled Sonny's head

and kissed little Casper on the nose. The pup never stirred and remained curled up in a ball.

Rhys and Sonny saw Sam off at the front door. She waved, blew Rhys another kiss and put her foot down to get to the hospital.

The woman on reception in the Accident and Emergency Department was getting abuse from a male patient about the length of time he'd been waiting to see a doctor. Her badge said *Helen*.

"I'm sorry, sir. I made you aware of the situation upon your arrival, and the sign is also prominent up there, that the waiting time is four hours."

"It's not good enough. I pay my taxes like everyone else around here, and this is what we've come to expect from people working in the NHS, to be treated like dirt."

Sam took a step forward and produced her warrant card. "Would you mind lowering your voice and calming down, sir? Helen has already explained the delay to you. In case you haven't read or seen the news lately, the NHS is grossly understaffed at present. It's up to all of us to have patience and consideration for those on duty, doing their very best under extreme circumstances. Now, go back to your seat and be a patient patient."

The room erupted with the sound of applause from the rest of the people waiting to be seen.

"Hear, hear," an older man shouted from the chair closest to the entrance. "None of us like hanging around here, but it is what it is. Get used to it or clear off home. You look all right to me. What's wrong with you?"

The enraged man's face grew redder. Sam feared he was about to vent his anger on someone else.

"Don't do it," she warned. "Go back to your seat and wait your turn."

He shuffled back on his injured leg, fell into his chair and glared at the man who had dared to challenge him.

"Thanks for that," Helen, the receptionist, said. "It's getting beyond a joke around here. The team are doing their best. It doesn't help that these patients can't get into their doctor's surgery at the moment, there are shortages across the board, and we're stuck with dealing with irate patients."

"I feel for you. I don't suppose all the strike action is helping, is it?"

"It hasn't. It's only going to get worse in the coming months. They announced today to expect more strikes in the next two months. It's lucky that I love my job. What can I do for you?"

"I'm here to see a Steve Palmer who was brought in with a knife wound a little while ago, from Workington, I believe."

"Let me check on the system for you, it's not a name I recognise as coming through here tonight."

"Oh God, don't tell me they transferred him to Carlisle right away."

"Bear with me. Ah yes, here he is. He must have come on the system while I nipped to the loo. One of the nurses watched the desk for me, she must have forgotten to mention it when I came back. Sorry for prattling on, he's in triage. Stay there, no, meet me at the door, I'll see you through." She pointed at the secure door over to the side.

"Thanks, see you over there."

Sam joined the smiling receptionist at the door.

Helen punched in a code and pulled one of the doors open. "Come on, I might as well take you down there myself as there's not another member of staff around."

"How do you cope with the level of abuse you get from the patients?"

"Most of the time I accept what they're saying with a smile set in place. I must admit that it's getting harder and harder, though. The strikes aren't helping, but then, some of the people who show up here shouldn't be here in the first place. That's due to the lack of GPs in the area. The NHS is rapidly going down the pan, and the government doesn't seem to give two hoots about it, and believe me, that's putting it mildly. I believe every MP should be forced to follow a member of staff around for a week, not a few hours, and not a consultant either. They should be forced to follow a nurse or an A and E doctor. They'd soon go back to parliament and want to change things. In my opinion, it's too late to action the changes, but I didn't say that. We'll keep doing our best for the patients who need us, most of whom are oblivious to the restraints we are under."

"Something has to give, eventually. We've got shortages throughout the police force but not a patch on what the NHS is suffering. You have my sympathy. Hey, if you get a lot of abuse, don't be afraid to give nine-nine-nine a call. We'll come up and sort them out for you."

"We used to have a security guard on duty, but he got made redundant a few years ago and has never been replaced. We had very little trouble back in those days. Maybe that's why they got rid of him."

"He was a deterrent, though, right?"

"Yep, short-sightedness at its best, now we're all suffering because of it."

Sam smiled. "I meant what I said, just give the station a call. There are always patrol cars in the area."

"I'll pass the message on to the other receptionists. Thanks for caring."

"Of course. What time do you finish tonight?"

"It should be ten, but I've said I'll do an extra hour as the girl taking over from me is out with her fella, celebrating their anniversary."

"You're a sweetheart, giving up your evening for her."

"I'd only be going home to bed, so no big deal. Here we are. If you wait here a mo, I'll pop my head around the door, see if one of the nurses or the doctor can spare you five minutes."

"Thanks for your help, Helen."

She smiled and entered a swing door. Sam paced the area for the next few minutes until Helen reappeared with a doctor by her side.

"This is Doctor Adebayo, he'll have a quick chat with you, Inspector." The receptionist left them and trotted back up the corridor to the reception area again.

"Hello, Doctor. I appreciate you having a word with me. I'm well aware how busy you are."

"I can only spare you a few seconds. The patient you're enquiring about was very lucky today. However, I doubt if he will see it that way."

"Would it be possible to have a quick chat with him?"

"I've given him pain medication. He keeps dozing off. He is conscious, though, so that's a blessing. I would ask that you don't hamper him for too long with your questions. Of course, he might refuse to see you, I haven't run it past him yet."

"I promise I'll be in and out. The last thing I want to do is put him under any kind of pressure."

"Good, I was hoping you'd say that. Come with me. I'll put you in a cubicle and get a porter to bring Mr Palmer to you."

Sam followed him to the cubicle area and sat in the chair next to the gap where the bed would be wheeled into, once Palmer arrived.

A few moments later, and the curtain was drawn back by a porter who said hello.

"Hi. Hello, Mr Palmer. How are you feeling?"

"Rougher than a cow's tongue," he replied, his voice

strained.

"Are you up to answer some questions?"

"Yes, I want to help the young woman, wouldn't want her being on my conscience."

"Very well. Did you get a good look at the man?"

"I did. He wasn't wearing a mask, if that's what you're getting at. It was quite dark when the attack happened. I was putting the rubbish out; it's bin day tomorrow, and I was shocked to see him attacking this young lady outside my house. He tried to make a joke about it, told me they were messing about. I didn't believe him one iota. The woman couldn't say anything because he'd put that silver tape over her mouth."

"You were very brave to tackle him. Most people would have turned their backs and closed the door on the situation."

"Brave? Maybe I was stupid, given the injury he's left me with. Another few centimetres and he would have got my heart. Fucker, who gives someone the right to attack another person like that?"

"I'm afraid most criminals are lacking in morals. I'm glad you're here to tell the tale. Are you going to have surgery?"

"The doctor said the wound wasn't deep enough, despite the amount of blood I've lost. He stitched me up and is sending me home in the morning. I'm not sure how I feel about that." He lowered his voice. "Bloody foreign docs, still not sure I trust them."

She raised an eyebrow. "We'd be lost without them serving us in the NHS. I take it you've heard about all the shortages the hospitals are experiencing at this time."

"Yes, there's no easy answer, I know. But I can't help wondering if I might have been treated better by a doctor from this country."

"Come now. Just because they're foreign, it doesn't mean they lack professionalism or qualifications."

"I know. Forget I said anything, I'm sorry."

"It's fine. Going back to the incident. What else can you tell me about the man?"

"He was skinny, and I spotted a scar on his face."

"Can you tell me where?"

"Above his right temple, I think. Yes, I'm sure it was on the right."

"That's significant, thank you."

"What are you saying, Inspector? That you know who this man is?"

"Yes, we believe he's struck before. We have two ongoing investigations where he has either attacked or abducted a woman."

He ran a hand over his face. "Oh shit! And what happened to the victims?"

"The first sadly didn't make it, and the second one we rescued yesterday, she's currently in hospital recovering from hypothermia. Please, don't worry about them, or the lady you tried to help. The criminal involved is very devious. However, he's in regular contact with us."

Palmer frowned and shook his head. "What? I don't understand. If you know who he is, why haven't you arrested him yet?"

"We don't. All we know about him at present is that he has a scar above his right temple."

"And how long has this been going on?"

"Since Monday. So not long, compared to other investigations I've dealt with over the years. We're clinging to the fact the man is in constant contact with us, hoping that he will slip up and that will lead to an arrest."

"And if it doesn't? How many more women will be killed or abducted?"

Sam shrugged. "I can't answer that. All I can do for now is try and keep the women alive until we rescue them. Believe me, in the meantime, my team are working like Trojans trying to track the culprit down."

"What about putting out a call to the public via one of those press conferences?"

"Already done at the beginning of the week. Nothing much came from it."

"Could you do another one? Now that he's struck again?"

"I'm seriously considering it. Still, that's my problem, not yours. I need you to get fit and well again."

"I don't think it will take long, nothing keeps me down. What about a statement?"

"Yes, we're going to need one, but not until you're well again."

"Just give me a shout. I want to do something to assist that poor woman. Right now I feel helpless and I detest the feeling."

"I know. You've done your best for now. If I can get your address and phone number, I'll pass it on to the desk sergeant. He'll make arrangements with you for one of his men to come out to see you at your convenience."

He gave her his details. Sam could tell by the way his eyelids were drooping that her visit had taken a lot out of him.

"I'm going to leave you to get some rest now. Thank you once again for at least trying to help save the woman. Sorry your heroism caused you to end up here, but I'm also relieved your injuries weren't worse."

"Thank you. I'd do it all over again if there was a miniscule chance of preventing someone from being kidnapped."

Sam smiled and held out her hand to shake his. "If only there were more people like you around, it would make our job so much easier."

"Good luck, Inspector."

She smiled again and left the cubicle. The porter was waiting outside.

"Thanks. I think he's tired and needs to rest now."

"I'll sort him, don't worry, Miss."

THE FOLLOWING MORNING, Sam gathered the team together. She had arrived at work at eight after dropping Sonny off at Doreen's earlier than usual. Her neighbour had shown concern for Sam, aware of how many hours she'd put in the day before. She had needed to assure Doreen that she was okay and that she would take some time off once they'd caught the bastard they were after.

"So, this is where we stand. It would appear the 'Changer of Lives'…"

"Or the bastard criminal as he's otherwise known," Bob interrupted.

"Yes, that as well," Sam agreed. "Whatever we prefer to call him, he's struck again. This time kidnapping a young woman out in the open. A man is in hospital; he tried to save the woman and got stabbed in the process. I paid him a visit as soon as I got the call last night. He gave me a brief description of the man, and yes, it would appear to be the same person."

"That's a relief," Bob replied, "Otherwise we could have two kidnapping perps in our midst."

Sam raised her eyebrow. "I'm sure we have a lot more than that in our midst, unfortunately. It's catching the buggers that is evading us at present. Therefore, I'm going to need you all to dig deeper, think and work harder than you ever have on any other case we've ever worked on. This fucker needs to be caught ASAP."

"Did this witness say anything else?" Bob asked. "By that, I mean did he get the make and model of the bloke's car? Was he on foot? Did he speak to him? Did he have an accent?"

"All valid questions. I really didn't want to hound the witness too much, he'd lost a lot of blood and was flagging a bit. All the relevant questions will be asked when an officer takes down the statement."

Bob nodded. "Fair enough. Where do we start looking on this one? He's clever, he knows that we'll be watching out for CCTV footage in the area. What else do we have to go on?"

"You're right, we shouldn't dismiss the cameras, if there are any in the area, and to be honest, we don't have a lot to go on, not until someone reports this woman missing. Claire, can you check the system for me? Not that I'm expecting anything to show up yet. It has to be worth a shot, though."

"I'll do that now, boss." Claire tapped at her keyboard and came up with the answer a few minutes later. "I've got a note on the system that a woman failed to return home after a night out with her friends. The husband rang the station but was told the usual, to make a report after twenty-four hours."

"Okay, if we have nothing else to go on, I think Bob and I should pay the husband a visit. If you can jot down the details for me, Claire."

She scribbled out the address and the man's phone number and handed it to Sam.

"Thanks, I'll give him a call before we set off."

"Have you checked your post yet?" Bob asked.

Sam shook her head. "Nope, not yet. I figured it was probably too soon for him to make contact with us."

"Probably. Might be worth a check, though?" Bob suggested.

"If there's nothing else anyone can think of that we've been missing, then yes, I'll go ahead and do that. Why don't you contact the husband for me, Bob?" She passed the details over to her partner and slipped into her office to check the post. As suspected, there was no sign of a note from the perpetrator, which put a slight doubt in Sam's mind.

Bob joined her a little while later and asked, "Turn that frown upside down, as my gran always used to say. What's up?"

"Nothing here."

"And? That's something to frown about? I thought you'd have erupted into your crazy dances by now."

"Firstly, I don't have any crazy dances in my repertoire, and secondly, what if this woman wasn't abducted by him? Are we going to assume every abduction is down to him? What about the dozens of other women who go missing every month on our patch?"

"That's a bit over the top. Want me to delve into the latest statistics of missing women in this area in the last year to prove a point?"

Sam screwed her nose up. "All right, smartarse. You don't have to take everything I say literally."

"Don't I? You mean I can pick and choose throughout the day? Can you imagine the hot water I'd get myself into if I turned around and did that?"

Sam heaved out a sigh. It was obvious she was fighting a losing battle with her partner. "Did you want something, Bob? Only I have this lot to go through, at my earliest convenience."

"Get you. Losing the battle of words, were you?"

She glowered and leaned back. "Time is marching on."

"Exactly. I contacted the husband, John Dakin. He's still very concerned about his wife. He's at work because he's self-employed and needs the money. I've told him we'll call in and see him this morning. He's going to be there all day, so I didn't set a specific time."

"Great, okay. Let me deal with this lot and then we'll pay

him a visit. And yes, another coffee would be a welcome addition to my day."

He grumbled as he left the office but nonetheless returned with a mug of coffee a few moments later. "Here you go, enjoy."

"I'm sure I will. Keep the team busy until I'm ready to go. I don't think I'll be too long."

"Take your time. Want me to chase up the lab as well?"

"You took the words out of my mouth."

"I'll get onto them now."

Sam knuckled down to answering a few emails she had neglected to answer the day before and then slit open the handful of brown envelopes littering her in-tray. All the while her thoughts lay with the latest victim and how distraught her husband was going to be. With that thought bugging her, she emptied her mug, shoved the unanswered letters back into the in-tray and slipped her jacket on once more.

Bob glanced up when she appeared in the doorway. He was on the phone and shaking his head at her.

She gestured for him to end the call. "Don't bother. Tell them you'll call back later. We should get going."

CHAPTER 9

John Dakin was a mess when they entered his shop. He was alone, working on the large machine behind the counter, cursing the contraption and hitting it as the frustration mounted.

"Mr Dakin?"

He turned to face them. "Damn, I'm so sorry, I didn't know anyone was in the shop, can't hear the bell once this thing starts up. Yes, how can I help? It's John by the way."

"Hello, John." Sam flashed her warrant card, and his eyes closed in what Sam could only think was relief. "I'm DI Sam Cobbs, and this is my partner, DS Bob Jones. You spoke to him earlier this morning, he told you to expect us."

"That's right. Hang on, I'll put the 'out for coffee' sign on the door to keep the punters out, not that there are a lot of them around lately. But that's another story."

He flew past them and dropped the latch on the shop door then instructed them to follow him into a stockroom out the back. "Excuse the mess, hard to find the time sorting out this crap when you're out there most days, dealing with customers."

"You own this business?"

"Yes, for over five years now. Can't say I'm making a living, not these days, but I get by. I'm still my own boss at the end of the day. Enough about my business, what about my wife? I was told that I couldn't file a report until the first twenty-four hours were up, that's not until this evening." He gasped. "Oh God, don't tell me you've found her... dead, have you?" He staggered backwards and gripped the bar of the shelving unit behind him for support.

"No, it's nothing like that, not in that sense." Sam glanced around, searching for a chair. "Bob, get that chair for John, would you?"

Bob leapt into action and placed the chair next to John.

"Take a seat, John."

"God. My legs have gone all weak now. What are you about to tell me?"

"That we believe your wife was possibly abducted last night. You told my partner that she was out with friends and the route she would likely have taken home. Well, at around nine last night, we received a call from a concerned member of the public, telling us that a woman was being abducted outside his house. As he made the call, the person stabbed him."

"Oh shit! Is he okay?"

"Yes, the wound turned out to be insignificant, however, he's still in hospital under observation as a precaution. He tried his hardest to prevent the attack. The abductor tried to tell him that he and the woman were role-playing."

"Sick shit! Tricia would never do anything like that, she isn't the type. Do you know who this man is?"

"We know of him but we've yet to identify him, mainly through lack of evidence at this stage. We believe he's the same culprit who has attacked two other women this week."

"Attacked? Don't you mean abducted?"

"Laying my cards on the table, not wishing to alarm you, but I feel I need to be upfront with you from the outset. The first victim was attacked, but she later died from her injuries."

"And the second?" he asked, his voice trembling.

"The second was abducted but later rescued by me and my team. She's safe. That's what I need you to cling on to."

"That's going to be hard when you've already told me that the first victim has already died. Why is he doing this? Do you know?"

Sam shook her head. "His motive thus far is a mystery to us. But we have forensic evidence we're analysing. Hopefully that will come through for us soon."

"And if it doesn't? Are you going to allow him to keep picking up innocent women, like my wife, from the streets? You should be out there now, searching for her. I think it's disgusting that I have been forced to wait twenty-four hours before I can even file a missing person report. How does that even work? This man could be miles away from here by now. Might have even sold her into the slave trade for all we know. You hear so many horror stories along those lines in the newspapers."

"How old is your wife, sir?"

"Thirty-five. Why? What does that have to do with anything?"

"It's just that if that scenario was on the table, it would have been dismissed by now."

"May I ask why?"

"Because your wife would be perceived as too old and would have very little value in the cut-and-thrust market of people trafficking."

"Oh right, well, that's a relief. Forgive me if I tell you that it doesn't allay my fears in any shape or form."

"I understand. Sorry, it was a silly thing for me to say."

"It's okay, I shouldn't have pushed or snapped at you. You're only trying to help me. I just feel so damn helpless. Is there anything I can do? What about one of those appeals to the public? Do you want me to stand in front of the camera and beg for this person to return my wife to me? Because I will if you think it will bring her home."

"To be honest with you, I don't think there's much point in putting a plea out there just yet. We need to be certain this person has taken her."

"I don't understand. The witness said that someone was abducting her. Whether it's the man you're after or not, there's no getting away from the fact that my wife is missing and someone appears to have taken her, presuming this woman was Tricia and not some other poor cow."

"Until we have more facts at our disposal, it's not something that I believe will benefit the case. That could change with a snap of my fingers, though. It takes time to set up a press conference, and right now, my priorities lay elsewhere."

His eyes narrowed, and he inhaled a large breath. "Why do I get the feeling that you're giving me the brush-off here, Inspector?"

"I'm not, I swear. What I haven't told you is that this person is in touch with me via letter. That's how we were able to rescue the second victim."

"What? Can't you trace his fingerprints through the letters?"

"We're trying. He's crafty, I believe he knows how to manipulate the system."

"What are you implying, that he's a copper?"

Sam shook her head. "Oh, no, I wasn't suggesting that at all. Let's face it, there are so many true crime programmes out there these days that we're finding the criminals are taking valuable notes and using them against us, if you like."

"Bloody hell. I hope that's not you coming up with an excuse as to why you haven't caught this person yet?"

"It's not. I'm not in the habit of using excuses with the victims' families during the course of an investigation. I'm sorry if it came across that way. May I ask what your wife does for a living?"

"She's a secretary at a legal firm in the centre of town."

The cogs started turning in Sam's mind. *Could there be a connection there? Was Tricia specifically targeted because of her job?*

"Inspector? I asked why you would want to know that information. Do you believe there could be a connection?"

"Possibly. It's something we need to delve into during our investigation. Can you tell me the name of the firm and where they're located?"

"Taylors and Sons in Arkwright Street. She's worked there for around five years or so."

"Has she mentioned having any problems with either her work colleagues or with any of the clients at the practice?"

"No, nothing that I can remember. Apart from…"

Sam's interest piqued. "Yes?"

"There was an incident with one of the solicitors about a month ago. She bumped the front of our car with his in the firm's car park. He went ballistic, told her that he'd only just bought the brand-new Merc and that he would send her the bill for the damage."

"What kind of damage are we talking about here, if she bumped it?"

"Exactly. She took a photo of the car. There was a single, two-inch scratch on the metal bumper. I couldn't believe he would rant and rave at her over such a minor knock. Nevertheless, he did. She was shaken up about the incident for a few days. It got so bad that I told her I'd go down there and sort it out with this jerk. She refused to let me get involved.

Told me that he was already making her life hell on the quiet, she really didn't want the problem to escalate any further."

"Does this jerk have a name?" Bob asked.

"Mr Forsyth."

"That will be our next port of call," Sam said. "Don't worry, we'll make it discreet when we have a word with him. Is there anything else you can tell us about your wife that you think will further our investigation?"

"I can't think of anything. Should I tell our family and friends? I haven't up until now."

"That's up to you. Maybe I would in your shoes, it might help to have some much-needed support at this time."

"Okay, I'll do that. Her mother is recovering from a hip operation, it's going to be hard sharing the news with her, she'll want to get out there, to search for her."

"There wouldn't be much point. I promise, as soon as the abductor contacts me, I will call you."

"You sound pretty sure that he is going to do that. Are you?"

"Going by past results, yes, I'm pretty sure."

"Let's hope you're right."

A knock on the front door steered his attention to his business once more. "I'd better get that. I have several customers dropping in for a few things I've made for them today."

"We're finished here anyway. I'll leave you my card. Give me a call if Tricia, or anyone else for that matter, gets in touch with you or if you think of anything else we should know."

"I'll do that. Please, do all you can to bring my wife home safely to me."

"You have my word," Sam replied, deep down hoping that would be the case.

He showed them back through to the shop, and Sam shook his hand.

He gripped it in both of his and held on to it longer than was necessary. "I hope you find her before this person hurts her, I mean does any lasting damage to her mental or physical health. That's my greatest fear, that she will come back a changed person."

"I get that. I'm sure we'll find her soon. She's our main priority, you can be sure of that."

They left the shop and wandered back to the car.

"It's all hard to fathom, isn't it?" Bob asked.

Sam unlocked the car doors, and they both slipped inside.

"Why's he targeting the women?" she asked.

"Yeah. None of it is making any sense to me."

"We still haven't worked out if there's a connection between the three victims or if the attacks were random. Until we do, there's no possible way we're going to solve this frigging investigation."

"Eek, that's not like you to be so negative, boss."

"I know. I've bitten my tongue more times than I care to mention but now I don't think there's any escaping the reality of the situation. This fucker has us by the short and curlies."

"I'm guessing that has been his intention all along."

Sam glanced sideways at her partner. "Care to elucidate, Bob?"

"Let's deal with the facts as we know them. Anyone could have stumbled across the first victim down at the park, but it was you who found her."

"Don't remind me. I have to live with that nightmare twenty-four hours a damn day."

"You think that was pure coincidence?"

Sam considered his question for some time before she responded. "Are you saying all this is about me?"

Bob shrugged. "Thinking outside the box because, let's face it, what else have we got going for us right now? Why not? Unless you want to share an alternative scenario with me?"

"I can't because I've yet to come up with one. But why?"

"Why not? It could be any number of things. You want me to start reeling them off while you take notes?"

"Sodding hell, don't say that."

He clutched his fingers to the palm of his hand and then pulled out his little finger and held it in his other hand. "First off, we could be looking at one of Chris's mates, keen to avenge his death."

"Get a life. That can't be right, surely."

He held up his hand again and gripped the next digit. "What about a family member of someone you've convicted recently?"

"Well, take your pick there."

"Or a con you banged up years ago, wanting revenge from inside?"

"Jesus, you've got a warped mind when you put it to good use. I'm not sure I like it when you put your thinking cap on… just saying."

He tutted but carried on all the same until all his fingers were covered with his other hand. "Or, going one step further, what about an ex-con you've put away in the past who has recently been given parole?"

Sam covered her face with both hands. "Stop! Don't you think I'm anxious enough about the investigation without you slinging this shit at me?"

"Sorry, all I was trying to do was assess the situation and come up with some plausible solutions. It's something we need to work on, isn't it? Or are you telling me that you think I'm way off the mark?"

"What I'm saying is… fucked if I know, because you clearly have all the answers."

Bob sighed and shrugged. "If you don't want to hear or even face up to the truth then I'll keep my trap shut."

"Is that a threat or a promise?"

"And you wonder why I prefer to keep my mouth shut when we're interviewing suspects."

Sam started the engine and drove off. A little while later she said, "All right, supposing what you said is true, where the heck do we begin looking?"

"I hadn't got that far."

"Backtracking a little, what if this guy saw me on the TV, requesting information about the first crime scene, and that got his back up enough to start messing with my head?"

"Maybe, but it still doesn't solve the issue of *you* finding the victim in the first place."

Sam growled. "You're right. Shit. Do you think I'm in danger?"

"I don't know, I think it would be foolish not to believe it."

"What about Rhys? Could he be in danger as well?"

Bob held up his hands and shrugged again. "Sam, I clearly don't have all the answers. Damn, I'm not even sure I have this partially right, but I think you need to take every precaution to keep yourself and those around you safe."

"Are you including yourself in that statement?"

"Possibly. Oh, I don't know. Once you start going over all the possibilities, the list could be endless. Maybe we should sit on the proposal for now and see where it leads us."

Sam drew up at the next set of lights and rested her head against the steering wheel for a few seconds. "Why does life have to be so damn complicated?"

"Someone up there is keen on testing us, that's for definite."

"I'd better run your suggestion past the chief. My life won't be worth living if he finds out that we've been mulling over the idea and failed to involve him."

"And what if I'm wrong?"

The lights turned to green, and Sam pulled away. "But what if you're right and we do nothing about it? I hate it… being put in this dilemma."

THEY ARRIVED BACK at the station a few minutes later. Sam had gone through all the reasons she shouldn't involve the chief and weighed them up against the reasons why she should, and they came up about even.

She branched off in the opposite direction at the top of the stairs. "I'll be back soon," she told Bob.

"Good luck."

"Thanks. Fill the team in during my absence. We'll bounce some ideas around when I get back."

Heidi glanced up from her computer as soon as Sam entered the room.

"Hi, Heidi. Is it convenient to have a quick chat with the boss?"

"Come in, he's always got time for you, Inspector. I'll have a word with him." She left her seat and tapped on the door to her right.

DCI Armstrong shouted for Heidi to join him.

She left the door open, choosing to dip her head around it. "DI Cobbs would like a quick word with you, sir."

"Okay, I'm pretty clear at the moment. No calls planned until later today, are there?"

"No, sir. I'll send her in. Can I get you a coffee? I'm sure the inspector would like one."

"Yes, that sounds like a great idea, Heidi, thank you."

Heidi stepped back and gestured for Sam to enter the room. "Coffee?" Heidi asked.

"I'd love one, thanks."

"I'll bring them in when they're ready."

"Hello, Sam. This is a surprise on a Saturday," the DCI said. "Looks like we're all working overtime to catch up on work."

"I wasn't sure if you'd be in today or not but then I spotted your car in your space and thought I'd drop by to see you. Umm… I could do with running something past you."

"Sounds ominous. Take your weight off your feet. Stop talking when Heidi comes back in, if you wouldn't mind."

"That's fine by me, sir." Sam sat and heaved out a sigh. "I don't know where to begin really."

Alan Armstrong linked his hands together and placed them on the desk in front of him. Sam began to talk, but he raised a finger when the door opened and Heidi brought in their drinks.

"That'll be all. I'll deal with it now, Heidi, thank you."

Heidi placed the tray with the two cups on the side of the desk and left the room.

Alan handed Sam her cup and saucer. She stared down at the rich dark colour, and the aroma of the fresh coffee beans had a somewhat calming effect over her that she had neither expected nor encountered before on a trip to the chief's office.

"You were saying? Has this got something to do with the investigation you're working on?"

"I believe so, sir." She ran through Bob's suggestion.

During her recapping of her partner's idea, the chief remained quiet and sipped at his drink. Once she'd finished, he turned his chair and took in the view out of his window, leaving Sam confused.

Sam didn't say anything further, just sipped at her own drink and bided her time.

"What if Bob is right about this? Do you have any indication who this person might be, who is keen on toying with you?"

"I haven't had a chance to sit down and make a list yet, sir."

He gave a short laugh before his face turned serious once more. "That many, eh? You need to make this your priority, Sam. If this criminal has you in his sights, then there's no telling what he's likely to do next or where this is going to end, if you get my drift?"

"I do, and the thought has gone round and round in my mind, sir. I need to sit down quietly, away from any distractions, and make a possible list of suspects. Even then, there's no guarantee I'll pin this bastard down. I'm on the news most weeks, at least I have been in the past year or so. Who's to say this person hasn't taken an instant dislike to me through the media?"

He shook his head over and over. "I've seen this type of thing before, where a killer has become obsessed with the SIO. What do we know about him?"

Sam snorted. "That he's slimly built and has a scar above his right temple."

His head jutted forward. "And that's it? Nothing from Forensics regarding the letters?"

"Zilch, absolutely nothing."

Alan blew out a frustrated breath and rested his head back against his chair. "Where do we go from here then?"

"I was hoping you'd be able to offer me some guidance on that because I really haven't got a clue."

"I feel for you, Sam, and if there's anything you can think of that you need to get you through this, don't hesitate to contact me, day or night."

Those are the exact words I say to a victim's family member after I've broken the bad news of their death. "Thanks, sir. I'll bear that in mind." She finished off her drink and rose from her seat. "I'd better go and thrash out some ideas with my team now. Enjoy the rest of your weekend."

"You, too. Try not to let things get on top of you. Reach out. I meant what I said, day or night, Sam."

Feeling deflated like a punctured dinghy, Sam left the office. On the way out, she thanked Heidi for the coffee.

"Aww… you're always welcome, Inspector."

Sam rejoined the rest of the team who were surprisingly quiet. "Who's died?" As soon as the words left her mouth, she regretted saying them.

"No one, as far as we know. We've all been sitting here, pondering what we can do to help you," Bob said.

Sam pulled up a chair and crossed her arms. "I'm dying… oh God, let me rephrase that, I'm eager to hear what you've come up with in my absence."

Bob's mouth twisted from side to side. "The problem is, we haven't, not really."

Again, Sam's mood sank to a lower level than she'd felt lately, even around Chris's death which had knocked her sideways. She jumped to her feet and walked towards her office. "I'll be in here if you want me." She firmly closed the door behind her and remained in that position for a while as the tears flowed freely. *What if Bob is right? There's no reason for me to dismiss his claims. But who? More to the point, why?* In need of hearing a friendly voice, she rang her sister, Crystal. "Hi, sis, how are you?"

"Umm… sorry, love, exceptionally busy at the moment. Can I give you a call back later?"

"Damn, it's Saturday. I forgot it's your busiest day of the week and the wedding season is virtually upon us. No problem. Love you."

"Hey, you sound down. Are you okay?"

"It'll pass. Go, speak to you later or tomorrow even."

"If you're sure. Love you back." Her sister was the one to end the call.

Then she rang Rhys—at least she began to dial his number but chickened out at the last minute. If Crystal had picked up on her mood, he was bound to do the same. Confused where to turn to or what to do next, Sam broke down. It was the only way she knew how to deal with the emotions overwhelming her. Luckily, her partner didn't feel the need to check up on her, like he usually did. Maybe he sensed her need to be alone right now.

Ten minutes later, she dried her eyes and took a swig from an unopened bottle of water she had lurking in her drawer, then left her office.

"I've got Claire doing her thing, going through all the cases we've solved in the past couple of years," Bob said. "Actually, we're all doing our bit. Liam and Oliver are trawling through the CCTV footage from the area of the latest abduction. They've found a couple of possible cars which could belong to the perp; they're doing some extra digging on that one. Suzanna is searching the database for crims with a scar above their right eye."

Sam smiled and gave him a hug, which was so out of character for her, he tensed up in her arms.

She released him and laughed. "Your face is a bloody picture."

"Touch me like that again and I'll put in a sexual harassment complaint."

Sam doubled over with laughter, and the rest of the team joined in.

"Hey, you think I'm joking? Do it and see the shit hit the fan."

Sam stood up straight and moved towards him.

He retreated a couple of steps and held his hand up, preventing her from coming any closer. "You've been warned."

"Party pooper. No, seriously, you guys are the best an inspector could have on his or her team. Where do we turn from here? More to the point, I expected the bastard to make contact with us by now. He hasn't, which begs the question, why not? Has he changed his MO to keep me or us on our toes?"

CHAPTER 10

The woman was pissing him off, crying all the time. Seeing the snot running down her face sickened him. He'd punished her several times since he'd abducted her, but instead of decreasing or ceasing altogether, her crying had intensified, driving his patience to the limits. He left the room, only to get the peace and quiet he needed to come up with a riddle to send Sam Cobbs.

Maybe I should ditch the idea altogether and just kill the bitch instead. That would solve a lot of problems rattling through my mind.

He put pen to paper as the ideas flowed now that he didn't have an emotional wreck in the same room as him.

The woman you're after is in need of your help.

I've punished her to within an inch of her life.

You better be quick if you intend to save her and return her to her life of misery.

We all have bridges to cross in this life, none greater than when our lives are in jeopardy.

Do you have it in you to take the leap of faith and rescue this bitch before she takes her final breath?

Waters run deep here, don't forget that snippet of information. But be quick, a rising tide and all that. Rain is forecast at the weekend. Will it be too late to save her?

Ask yourself if you have it within you to conquer your fears and save her, Inspector Cobbs.

GARNER PUNCHED the air in jubilation, pleased with his accomplishment. Now all he had to do was find a passerby willing to deliver the note to the station, unless… Another plan entered his mind, and he beamed. Then he went one step further and danced around the kitchen. "I really am a sick fucker at times."

He filled the kettle and prepared cheese on toast for them both, not bothered in the slightest if she ate hers or not. He was ravenous by his exertions. She had been a handful to deal with so far, but that was about to change. He had something special planned for her, and she'd need to keep her strength up for the challenge that lay ahead.

While he waited for their supper to cook, he went in search of the miner's lamp he had tucked away under the stairs, along with a mountain of other junk he stored under there. Halfway through the search the smoke alarm went off in the kitchen. He bolted in there to find their supper ablaze under the grill. The woman screamed in the lounge. He tore in there and smacked her in the mouth. Her head flopped forward; she was out cold. He cursed under his breath and returned to tackle the blaze. He hadn't intended to hit her quite so hard. Still, what's done is done, no going back now. Once he dealt with the fire, he'd throw a cup of water in her face to revive her.

He switched the alarm off, but it started up again. In a fit of rage, he yanked it off the ceiling and removed the battery from the back. The silence was the relief he needed to combat the fire. "What a bloody waste. That was the last of the cheese, too. I'll need to take a trip out now. It can wait until later. Once my plan is sorted in my head, I can kill two or three birds with one stone, so to speak." His head tipped back, and he laughed.

He threw the grill pan in the sink and ran the cold water over the blazing food. The flames died down instantly, and he returned to the lounge to check on the woman.

"Oh, Tricia, wake up now. All the danger has been snuffed out. We're fine now. It's safe to come around again." He shook her shoulders.

Tricia moaned and raised her head to look at him. "Why did you hit me?"

"Umm... because there's no one here to prevent me from doing what I want, when I want. Are you hungry?"

"No, not any more. Please, let me go home, my husband will be going out of his mind with worry."

"Tough. Like I care. Starve then. I keep telling you, if you don't eat you won't survive the battles and challenges that lie ahead of you. Do you like to fail? Most women don't care a jot if they fail or not. Most of them latch on to a strong male instead of fending for themselves in this life. Shame on them. You fought for equality all those years ago. To see it diminish and fail must have Emily Pankhurst, or whatever her name was, probably turning in her grave now."

"It's Emmeline," she corrected him.

He grabbed her round the throat with both hands and squeezed until her eyes bulged, and then he released his grip. Her head fell backwards, and she gasped for breath.

"Why?" she pleaded. "Why are you doing this to me? I don't know you. As far as I know our paths have never crossed. Or have they?"

He smirked and touched his forehead against hers. "That's for me to know. I'm sick of speaking to you. We need to go out soon, we'll just wait a little longer until it gets dark."

"No, I don't want to go out there. What are you going to do to me?"

"You'll find out soon enough, don't fret. I won't leave you in the dark for too long." He chuckled at his own joke.

Tricia simply stared at him, contempt etched into her features. He swooped and sank his teeth into her cheek. Shocked, she cried out.

Laughing, Garner left the room and continued his search in the cupboard for the lamp. He discovered other useful things that used to belong to his father while he hunted through the boxes. Setting the items aside, he crawled on his hands and knees to get further into the cupboard. He tore open a box wedged into the pointed area at the rear and shouted, "Bingo! By Jove, I've finally found it." Removing the lamp from the box, he checked to see if it worked. He remembered it never failing his father back in the day.

He walked back out into the hallway and did another jig around the cramped area with his lamp in his hand. "I've got my lamp, I can do anything I want to. Get to places off the beaten track in the dead of the night. Let the games begin, Sam Cobbs, you're not going to know what has hit you now."

CHAPTER 11

"I found this letter on your windscreen." Rhys waved the envelope in front of Sam's face.

She had been nice and relaxed with the dogs on the sofa. She jumped up and shouted at him to drop it then ran into the hallway to search through her pockets for a glove.

"What's going on? What are you doing?" he called after her.

She returned and snapped her gloves on. "It's probably from him. In future, you should call me and never handle anything that has been left for me."

His eyes widened. "I didn't think. Of course I shouldn't, because of the forensic side of things, right?"

"Yes. I'm sorry I shouted at you. I need to read this, it can only be bad news."

"I'll give you some room and take the boys in the garden."

Sam smiled and nodded. "Thanks."

After Rhys and the boys left the room, she closed the door and sat on the edge of the sofa, staring at the note. *He came here! He left the note where he knew it would be found quickly, well, in the morning at the latest.*

She shuddered at the thought of the killer being within a few feet of Rhys, the dogs, and even Doreen, her neighbour. "What if...? No, I can't think like that. I won't allow this fucker to screw with my head."

She opened the envelope and removed the note.

THE WOMAN *you're after is in need of your help.*

I've punished her to within an inch of her life.

You better be quick if you intend to save her and return her to her life of misery.

We all have bridges to cross in this life, none greater than when our lives are in jeopardy.

Do you have it in you to take the leap of faith and rescue this bitch before she takes her final breath?

Waters run deep here, don't forget that snippet of information. But be quick, a rising tide and all that. Rain is forecast at the weekend. Will it be too late to save her?

Ask yourself if you have it within you to conquer your fears and save her, Inspector Cobbs.

"SHIT! SHIT! SHIT!"

She ran into the kitchen. Rhys was drying the dogs' feet by the back door.

"I'm sorry. I've got to go. This woman's life is in danger, and I would never be able to forgive myself if I sat around here and did nothing to help."

"While I agree with you, surely you must have someone you deem reliable down at the station who can deal with a major issue in your absence."

She shook her head. "Only my team and I should be involved in this. I'm sorry if this has spoilt your... our evening, but I can't sit back and ignore that this woman's life is in imminent danger. I've wasted enough time already."

"How do you work that one out?"

"I have no idea how long the note has been out there."

"It's only just got dark. I can't see him coming here unless he used the darkness as a shield."

"You're probably right." With Rhys being a logical thinker, she opened the note and laid it out on the table. "Don't touch it. What do you make of it?"

He finished wiping Casper's paws, gave the dogs a treat and hung the towel up on the rail to dry before he even got around to approaching the table, which annoyed Sam.

"Give me five minutes," she said. "I'm going to see how many members of my team I can round up."

"Good luck with that. It's Saturday night, or had you forgotten?"

"No, I hadn't." She rang Bob first. "Hey, it's me. Have you been drinking?"

"I've had a glass of wine. I was about to pour another glass, why?"

"I need the team to meet up at the station. I've heard from the killer. He's given me another riddle, her life is in imminent danger. If we don't put our heads together tonight, she's going to die."

"Fuck. I'll meet you there. What about the others?"

"I haven't tried them yet, I thought I would give you a call first. See you at the station."

Rhys glanced up from the note and raised an eyebrow. "And you're expected to know the location from the clues he's given?"

"Yep. He doesn't make things easy, does he?"

"Want me to scan the map, see if any locations come to mind?"

"While I ring the rest of my team? That would be great, Rhys."

"It's the least I can do. Saves me standing around twiddling my thumbs, thinking I'm a waste of space."

She dialled the next number and ran a hand around his face. "You could never be that. Yes, Liam, it's Sam, sorry to disturb your evening. Have you had anything to drink?"

"Umm… one can of beer, boss. What's up?"

"I'm contacting all the team to see if you guys are up for joining me back at the station."

"Ouch, can I ask why?"

"I've heard from the killer. I think he's dumped the woman somewhere. Looks like we have another treasure hunt on our hands."

"Damn. I'll get to the station ASAP. Want me to call Oliver?"

"If you wouldn't mind. Thanks, Liam, I owe you one."

"It's all in a day's work, boss."

She ended the call and ran through the names of the rest of her team. She managed to get hold of everyone bar Alex, whose phone was apparently switched off.

By now, Rhys had laid out an OS map of the Lake District on the table and was highlighting a few interesting locations.

Sam handed him a pen. "Can you circle them? I'll need to leave soon. Thanks for all your help, Rhys."

"I haven't done anything, not really. You guys are the ones who are going to be the real heroes, when, not if, you track this woman down. I wish I could be more involved. My adrenaline is pumping. I think I understand why you do what you do now, Sam."

"There are the mundane parts of the job to consider, too, before you think about signing up for the force."

He laughed. "I bet."

"I must crack on." She continued to ring the rest of the

team. Her heart swelled with joy when they all agreed to join her back at the station. Even though they were probably as exhausted as her after what they'd had to contend with over the past seven days, no one let her down, well, only Alex. Knowing him, he'd switched off his phone on purpose while he exercised his arm down at his local boozer. "That's a relief. Only one team member down, I'll take that."

"They're a good bunch. They must think a lot of you to want to give up the start of their weekend."

"They're a class act. I'm thrilled to work alongside them every day. Not every inspector or DCI can spout those words, I can tell you. I need to go. Appreciate your help. At least it's given us somewhere to start." She kissed him and patted both dogs on the head then raced to the front door, the dogs tearing along the hallway after her, expecting to go for an extra walk. "Sorry, guys. Have a cuddle with your dad instead."

Rhys called them, and they trotted happily back to him. "They'll be fine. You worry too much. Ring me later, if you get the chance."

"I will. Thanks for being so understanding about this, Rhys. I'll make it up to you when this case is over."

"There's no need. I quite enjoy living with a real superhero."

She chuckled. "I'm hardly that, but thanks for the compliment."

Sam left the house and jumped into the car. She flashed her lights at Doreen who had pulled back her curtain, probably wondering what all the commotion was about. Doreen waved and blew her a kiss.

The drive back into town was made through several downpours. She felt grateful that the weather had held off long enough for Rhys to retrieve the note before it got washed away.

Sam tore through the main entrance of the station and up the stairs to the incident room where most of the team had already assembled and helped themselves to a coffee.

"I'll get you one, boss," Claire said.

"Who are we waiting for? Alex won't be joining us as I couldn't get hold of him."

"There's a surprise." Liam sniggered. "Just waiting on Suzanna and Bob to arrive now."

Sam removed the map from inside her jacket and laid it on the nearby desk. Claire handed her a mug of coffee. Sam asked her to put on a pair of gloves and then gave her the note.

"Can you run off a few copies for me?"

Claire nodded and crossed the room to the printer. She switched it on, waited a few seconds for it to warm up, then printed off the copies and returned to the group. By this time, Bob and Suzanna had arrived. Liam fixed them a coffee.

"First of all, I want to thank you for giving up your Saturday evening. You know I wouldn't request your attendance unless it was some kind of emergency. As you can see, the killer delivered a note to me this evening."

"Wait, where? Not at your house?" Bob demanded.

"Yep, he left it on my windscreen."

"Shit. I know I suggested that this person probably knows you but... well, this backs up that theory and then some. What does the note say?"

Sam laid the copies on the map for the others to read for themselves and tucked the original back in the envelope which she was keeping in an evidence bag, then she removed her gloves.

"As you can see, Rhys and I have already highlighted a few possible locations. Feel free to throw in any extra ones that come to mind after reading the riddle."

"Bridges, prominent bridges," Bob muttered over and over.

"It could be any of them. Every river has to have a bridge over it, doesn't it?" Liam asked.

"That's what's troubling me," Sam admitted. "Therefore, we need to sort through the other clues he's given us to narrow it down."

"He mentions leap of faith, could he be talking about a waterfall?" Liam asked. "Waters run deep, another point to a waterfall, maybe, as opposed to a normal bridge crossing a river."

Sam scoured the map, and she pointed at one particular area. "What about here, it's doable, not too far, around forty to forty-five minutes. Of course, I have no way of knowing what time he left the note or dumped the woman at the location."

"Lingcove Bridge and waterfalls. It's got to be worth the gamble. Wait, there's another possibility close by, the Stanley Ghyll Waterfall at Eskdale. Looks like they're within ten to fifteen minutes of each other. Might be worth us splitting up and tackling both locations at the same time, what do you reckon?" Bob suggested.

"If that's what you think, I'm ready to back you a hundred percent, Bob. Does anyone else have any other proposals?"

The team kept their gazes glued to the map, but no one was willing to offer up any alternatives.

"If we're all agreed, I think we should head off. I'm going to speak to the desk sergeant first, see how many men he can spare us." Sam slipped into her office to make the call and was delighted when the sergeant informed her he had eight uniformed officers available and they were downstairs waiting, having just attended a meeting about new procedures.

Sam arranged the teams when they reached the reception area. She and Bob would be joined by Suzanna. While Liam,

Oliver and Claire, who insisted she should fill in for Alex this time, would follow in Liam's car. Four patrol cars with eight uniformed officers would accompany them.

FORTY MINUTES LATER, they arrived at Boot. Sam, Bob and Suzanna opted to go to Lingcove Bridge and sent the other team up to Eskdale.

"Keep in regular contact, guys. As usual, don't take unnecessary risks. Stay safe. We'll contact you if we find the woman at the falls. Don't forget, her name is Tricia Dakin. Make sure you call out her name often, if only to let her know you're in the area, searching for her. Right, let's get this show on the road. Good luck."

Sam and the team had to set off on foot, and in patches, they found the terrain less than forgiving in places.

"This area is vast. Where the fuck do we begin the search?" Bob complained.

Sam sighed. "I haven't got a clue. I suppose we should head for where the river is at its deepest."

"That could be anywhere along this stretch."

"If I might make a suggestion, ma'am," one of the younger officers accompanying them said, "I come here quite often with my family. There's a large pool area just up here on the left, which is pretty deep, and it's at the base of the waterfall."

"Do you think you can find it in the dark?" Sam asked. She scanned the darkness ahead of them, already regretting her decision to come out here at this time of night, risking their own lives in trying to rescue the woman.

"I'll give it a try, ma'am."

The uniformed officer led the way. They were halfway up a steep path when Sam's radio crackled and Liam's voice boomed out.

"DI Cobbs, we've found her. Are you receiving me? I repeat, we've found Tricia Dakin."

"Thank God. Well done, guys. Is she okay?"

"Cold. We found her half-naked. She's relieved to have been rescued."

"That's good enough for me. We'll meet you back in Boot. She'll need to be rushed to the hospital."

"We're setting off now. We're not too far from the car, about fifteen minutes. I'll carry her back to the vehicle."

"You're a treasure, Liam. See you soon."

He clicked his radio twice in response.

"Thank fuck for that," Bob said as he exhaled a large breath. "Things were about to get hairy up ahead. If it had all been in vain, I wouldn't have been a happy chappy."

Sam turned her back on him and mumbled, "So what's new? Come on, guys. All's well that ends well. Thanks for all your efforts anyway."

THEY MET up with the other team thirty minutes later. Sam introduced herself to Tricia Dakin, and they transferred the woman to Sam's car. She told Suzanna to head back with the rest of the team, and she and Bob drove Tricia to Whitehaven hospital.

She handed her keys over to Bob to drive while Sam comforted Tricia in the back seat. "Shall we give your husband a call? He's been anxious about you."

"Yes, please." Tricia sniffled, pulled the blankets around her shoulders and clutched them at her chest. "I'm so cold. Why did he kidnap me, do you know?"

"I don't. I was hoping you'd be able to shed some light on that for us."

"I didn't recognise him. I don't think I know him. Saying that, I was scared shitless most of the time." She rubbed her cheek. "He was vile. He bit me a number of times, as if that would keep me in control." Her chin dropped.

Sam got closer and whispered, "Did he harm you in any other way?"

Tricia turned to face her, and with tears bulging, she nodded. "Yes, he raped me. I don't think I'll ever let another man touch me for as long as I live."

"It'll be okay. We'll make sure you get all the help you need in the form of counselling. We won't desert you in your hour of need, I promise."

Sam then made the call to John Dakin. "John, it's DI Sam Cobbs. I've got good news for you."

"Oh God, please tell me you've found Tricia."

"We have. We're on our way to Whitehaven hospital. Do you want to join us there?"

"Of course. I'm leaving now. How long will you be? Is she all right?"

"About thirty minutes. She's safe and well. A little bruised and battered, but she's in good spirits." Sam winked at Tricia who nodded in agreement.

"Thank you so much. Will you be at the hospital when I arrive?"

"We'll hang around, don't worry. Go directly to the Accident and Emergency Department when you get there."

"Thanks, I'll do that. See you soon."

Sam ended the call.

Tricia leaned her head on Sam's shoulder and whispered, "Thank you, for everything. Most of all for not giving up on me."

"Never, it's not in my remit to give up on people in need of our help. You're going to be fine. I can see how strong you are. Try to rid yourself of the evil images that man has embedded in your mind and think of the positives. You're alive and you're going home to be with your husband. Well, via a necessary trip to the hospital."

"Thank you," Tricia whispered again.

Sam caught Bob eyeing her in the rear-view mirror and smiled at him. He returned the smile and put his foot down once they reached the A595.

THE RECEPTIONIST on duty was Helen. "Back again so soon, Inspector. Who do we have here?"

"Would it be all right if we discuss this in a private room? This woman needs to be seen right away."

"'Ere, I heard you. We'll have none of that queue-jumping, not when I've been waiting five hours to be seen," a large man shouted from behind Sam.

Here we go again! Same old crap from yet another angry patient waiting to be seen.

"Pipe down," Bob warned. "Or I'll arrest you for disturbing the peace."

"If she gets seen before me, you'd better lay a bloody assaulting a police officer charge at my door as well, mate. You lot don't scare me."

"I don't want to make a fuss," Tricia mumbled.

"You're not," the receptionist said. "Come to the end. I'll get you into triage out of the way."

Sam and Bob rushed Tricia through the reception area to the secure door at the end. The man could be heard ranting and cursing behind them.

"Let me deal with this knobhead first," Bob said.

Sam latched on to his arm. "Ignore him."

Instead of lumping the man one, Bob gave him one of his intense glares that had the desired effect of shutting up the outspoken idiot.

"Some people just aren't worth the aggro," Helen whispered. She punched in the code and led the three of them into the triage area. "You'll be safe here. I'll have a word with someone then I'll have to get back to the mayhem out there."

Sam smiled. "I can't thank you enough for looking after us so well, Helen."

"Don't mention it. We're part of the team, aren't we?"

"We are. Thanks again."

She trotted back up the corridor. The same doctor who'd dealt with Sophie, emerged from the triage area and whisked Tricia away to check her over. Her husband, John, appeared a few minutes later. Another member of staff collected him and took him to be with his wife. Sam and Bob paced the area and drank coffee until it came out of their ears for another couple of hours before the doctor reappeared and apologised for not getting back to them sooner. He'd admitted Tricia to the Women's Ward and told Sam to let her rest overnight and to ring the ward in the morning to see if she was up to speaking with her.

Deflated, Sam drove Bob back to the station to pick up his car, and they both headed home at gone one in the morning after completing their paperwork and statements regarding Tricia. Sam's head felt like mush as she toppled into bed beside Rhys. He stirred and flung a lazy arm over her and pulled her in close for a cuddle.

"I love you," he whispered.

"I love you, too. We found the woman."

Snoring greeted her instead of the expected jubilation she was hoping to hear from him. Sam drifted off to sleep not long after.

CHAPTER 12

Sam was up with the birds the following morning. One glance in the mirror, and she cringed at the black circles around her eyes and the creases in her skin that seemed to have materialised overnight. "You're getting old, girl. All this traipsing around over uneven terrain in the dead of the night to save someone isn't helping either."

She'd left the door to the bathroom ajar, and Rhys pushed it open and leant against the doorframe.

"Is that you talking to yourself?"

"I'm talking to someone I no longer recognise as me in the mirror, does that count?"

He laughed. "It's all a figment of your imagination. In my eyes, you're still the beautiful woman who attracted me at the bridge."

"Get out of here."

"Sorry I was fast asleep when you came home. I tried to stay up but I suppose exhaustion took over. Did you find the woman?"

"Yes, we did great. We figured out where she was and split into two teams. The other team found her not long after we began our search, thankfully. I dread to think how long she would have lasted out there if they hadn't. She was half-naked and scared shitless. Bob and I dropped her off at the hospital. I need to chase that up this morning. See if she's up to speaking with me."

"Oh, I was hoping we would be able to spend the day together with the dogs. Do some light training with Casper and maybe go for Sunday lunch somewhere."

She touched his cheek. "We probably still can. Let me ring the hospital first and go from there."

"Okay. Want some toast and coffee? I need to let the boys out. I might as well make it while I'm down there. We can have breakfast in bed for a change."

"Sounds wonderful. I'll ring the hospital and check on Tricia while you do all that. Thanks for being you, Rhys."

"Meaning?"

"Meaning, for not blowing up when I mention putting work first on what is supposed to be my day off."

"Don't worry about it. I fell in love with your caring side as well as you as a person."

They shared a kiss. Sam watched him leave and completed her bathroom routine before she rang the hospital. The nurse informed her that Tricia had finally dropped off to sleep at around four after having a restless night. Sam told her that she would call back around lunchtime to check how Tricia was doing then and possibly visit her in the afternoon. The nurse agreed that would be for the best.

Rhys appeared a few minutes later with a bulging breakfast tray full of goodies she had no idea existed in her house.

"Croissants? Where did these come from?"

"I brought them on the way home yesterday and hid them in the cupboard. Tuck in while they're still warm. I bought a pot of homemade strawberry jam from the baker's at the same time."

Breakfast was delicious, and they spent the next five minutes discussing how to spend the rest of the day, what pub to drive to for lunch, with one proviso, that Sam checks in on the hospital early afternoon.

Rhys was happy to agree if it meant them spending time together as a family with the dogs.

AFTER TUCKING into a large roast dinner at the White Swan on the outskirts of Workington, Sam rang the hospital and was told she could visit Tricia for a maximum of ten minutes. She jumped at the chance. Rhys drove her to the hospital and waited in the car with the dogs while she ran through the corridors to the Women's Ward. She produced her ID at the nurses' station, and the younger of the two nurses showed her down the ward to Tricia's bed. Her husband was sitting alongside her, holding her hand.

"Hello, there. How are you feeling today?"

"Oh, hello, Inspector. I suppose as well as can be expected, in the circumstances. I didn't have a good night," Tricia replied, her voice strained with emotion.

"I'm sorry to hear that. I did call earlier to see how you were, and the nurse told me you didn't get to sleep until about four. It will get easier, I promise you."

Her husband snorted. "Will it? You think her life, *our* lives, are ever going to be the same again?"

"In time. I'm not denying that your wife has been through a horrendous ordeal but I can see she's a strong-willed lady who will get through the other side."

"Forgive me, but do you have a crystal ball or something similar? How can you tell that when she has just cried on my shoulder, telling me that she fears she will never get over what that man put her through? Talking of which, have you caught the bastard yet?"

Sam inhaled a large breath. "No, I don't have a crystal ball, but my considerable experience has shown me that women are resilient in these types of cases and nine times out of ten surprise friends and family with how well they seem to get on with their lives."

"Seem to?"

"We can offer your wife counselling, she only has to ask."

"And, have you caught him yet? Or is he still out there? Scouring the streets for his next victim? I hear Tricia isn't the only woman this no-mark has attacked this week. The rumour mill is rife around here."

"No, we haven't. But I can assure you that we're closing in on him."

"Closing in on him? Do me a favour, stop lying, Inspector. Why don't you admit you don't know who this man is?"

"We're awaiting the results of the tests carried out on evidence found at several crime scenes. Your wife's clothes were sent directly to the lab; we hope to have the results within a few days. That doesn't mean that we will be sitting on our hands until we get them. We have a few avenues open to us to explore."

"Now I know you're giving me some kind of spiel they probably tell you to say down at the police academy. Don't you want this bastard caught?"

Tricia gripped her husband's hand. "John, you promised me you wouldn't do this. I can't handle all this stress, not now."

"I'm sorry, love. I'm just frustrated. She shouldn't be here, she should be out there, trying to find this fucker."

Tricia raised an eyebrow, and her husband lifted her hand to his mouth and kissed the back of it.

"I'm sorry, I'll wash my mouth out when I get home. This guy has got me so riled up..."

"It's understandable, Mr Dakin," Sam said. "Believe me, I

feel the same way as you do. My team and I are desperate to get this man behind bars."

"So why aren't you out there now?"

"Because I wanted to drop by and check on your wife and ask her a few questions, if she's up to it."

"I'm fine. Excuse my husband, Inspector, he tends to blow things up out of all proportion. He means well."

Her husband released her hand and crossed his arms. "Pardon me for caring. I won't bother in future."

"Now you're being ridiculous. Why don't you go and get yourself a coffee while I have a chat with the inspector?"

"And now you want me out of the way?" He jumped to his feet and tore out of the cubicle.

Sam winced. "I'm so sorry, I didn't mean to cause any trouble between you."

"You haven't, don't worry. Please, let's get the questions over and done with before he cools off and returns only to get irate again to find you still here."

"As you wish. I wondered if you either knew the man or had seen him anywhere before."

"No, not to my knowledge."

"Did he either tell you or hint at why he abducted you?"

"I asked him, he refused to tell me. I got the impression that I was there for the taking. He was prowling the streets with the intention of abducting someone. Is it right, what you said, about not knowing who he is?"

Sam sighed. "Sadly, that's true. Like I told your husband, we're awaiting the results of the evidence. If they find any then we can cross-match it with our system."

"Do you keep everyone's DNA profile in the system? Is that how it works?"

"No, it will only show a result if the man has already been arrested."

Tricia slapped a hand to her face. "And if he hasn't? Are you telling me you will never be able to find him?"

"No, we never say never. My team and I have a ninety-eight percent success rate, so you must never give up on us."

She shook her head and closed her eyes. "Thinking back, not that I want to, but he made a point of wearing gloves all the time. I thought it was strange but I understand completely now why he did it."

"He's devious, appears to know all our police procedures. Did he use a condom?"

"How does he know? Yes, he used one."

"Unfortunately, it's something we come up against daily. There are so many programmes and dedicated TV channels which cover true crimes, the information is out there for all to see. However, saying that, nine times out of ten these criminals slip up, and that's what generally leads to their arrest."

"So you're telling me it's a waiting game?"

"Possibly. Which is why anything you can tell me, no matter how insignificant you think that would be, might help us."

"And if I can't tell you anything then you're saying that he's going to be allowed to strike again, is that it?"

Sam sighed and hitched up a shoulder. "I hope not, but there is little I can do to guarantee it. He seems to carry out the attacks, or abductions, in areas where there are no CCTV cameras available."

Tricia shook her head and covered her face with her hands and sobbed. "But he can't be allowed... not to rape someone else. Someone has to prevent it from happening again."

Sam sat in the chair not long vacated by the husband and placed a hand over Tricia's. "Please don't upset yourself. As I said, we're going to try our best to ensure that doesn't happen."

"But you can't guarantee it, they were your exact words. I feel sick at the thought of another woman going through the trauma I went through. No one has the right to violate someone, to rob them of their self-worth."

Before Sam could answer, the curtain flew open again and John Dakin appeared. He took one look at how upset his wife was and pointed at Sam.

"Out, get out and leave us alone. I won't have my wife upset further. Get out of here before I call security and get you escorted out."

"John. Please, she's only doing her job," a distraught Tricia pleaded.

"She can do that back at the station, without hounding you for the answers. If she's not up to the job then she should admit it, not come down here and bombard you with questions when you're at your lowest ebb. That's my final word on the subject. Now get out!"

A nurse appeared. "I'm only going to tell you this once. You need to keep the noise down, other patients on this ward are entitled to their rest. I think it's time you were leaving, Inspector."

"Hooray, I've been telling her that myself," John was quick to add.

Sam jumped out of her seat. She removed a card from her pocket and handed it to Tricia. "Ring me if you think of anything or just need to chat."

Her husband went to snatch the card from her grasp, but Tricia held it against her chest.

"She gave it to me, not you. I'm sorry, Inspector. Thank you again for rescuing me. I doubt if I would be here today if it wasn't for the bravery of your team. It would seem some people around here have very short memories regarding what I've been through in the last forty-eight hours."

Sam smiled and squeezed past the husband. She felt the waft of his steaming breath on her cheek as she passed. "Goodbye. Glad you're safe and well, Tricia."

Sam trudged back to the car and jumped in beside Rhys.

He placed his hand over hers and asked, "Hey, are you all right?"

"I just want to go home and chill out on the sofa. I'm fed up with working myself up into a tizzy through exhaustion only to be slapped down by unappreciative relatives."

"What the...? No way. I'm so sorry this has happened to you, Sam. No one works harder than you to solve an investigation. People suck. Come on, we'll stop off at a pub on the way home. The dogs can join us. I'm not having you doubt your ability. Shame on the person doing the slapping down, ungrateful..."

"It's okay. He's entitled to his opinion. I know he's talking out of his arse, it just gets to me sometimes."

SAM HAD a thick head from the alcohol she had consumed at the pub the previous day. She'd only had a few drinks, compared to others, but for someone out of practice, even two full glasses of wine were enough to send her squiffy.

She joined the others in the incident room and was busy dishing out the praise and going over what she had encountered at the hospital when Claire answered the phone on her desk.

"Yes, she's here. Hold the line."

Sam faced her, and her eyebrows pinched into a frown. "Who is it?"

"Sorry, I got the impression he wasn't going to tell me. I think it might be him, boss."

Sam marched across the room, the ache in her head temporarily forgotten about, and grabbed the phone. "DI Sam Cobbs, how may I help?"

"You found her then. Didn't take you long this time. Either my clues are lacking or you're thinking along my lines, Sam."

"What do you want from me? Who are you? Do I know you?"

Her questions were greeted with silence. She strained her ear and, after a while, heard him catch his breath.

"I do, don't I? Leave the women out of this. If you have a problem with me, sort it out with me and stop involving innocent members of the public."

He laughed. "Where would the fun be in doing it your way? I much prefer to be in control, it gives me the upper hand."

"Where do we know each other from? At least tell me that."

"Your problem is that you want everything handed to you on a plate, Sam, you always have."

Sam tried hard to rack her brains, but recognising his voice was nigh on impossible. "Meet me in person. Be a man about this and take me on, stop abducting other women when clearly your gripe is with me."

"There you go again, always keen on dishing out the orders, even when they're not needed. Our paths will cross one day, don't worry about that."

"When? Why not now? What are you waiting for? We're closing in on you," she added and immediately bit down on her tongue for telling the big fat lie.

"Don't make me laugh, how could you be? You've just told me you don't know who I am. Stop treating me like an idiot, Sam. You should have more respect for people, especially if they have the advantage, like I do. You've always…"

"Always what? Come on, if you've got something to say, let me hear it."

"It'll keep. Not long to wait now. But first, I have another special game for you to play."

"What are you talking about? Don't tell me you've abducted someone else?"

"Okay, I won't, except I'd be lying."

"Who is she? Where did you abduct her from? What are your intentions?"

"Questions, questions, questions. You always were a nosey bird, back in the day. I couldn't even have a shit... no, scratch that. Loose lips sink ships." He laughed and hung up.

Sam was seething. Claire had tried to run a trace on the call, but it was as though he knew what he was doing and hung up before a result could be found.

"Nothing, sorry, boss," Claire apologised.

"It's not your fault. It's mine, I pushed him too much and too hard. Shit, shit, shit. He's abducted another woman. I'm presuming this was after he dropped Tricia off on Saturday. So we need to check the system, see if a woman has been reported missing either Saturday from around three or yesterday. Bugger, why didn't I keep him talking? Worm the information out of him?"

"You did your best, boss. I'll check the system now."

"Thanks, Claire. Oliver, can you contact the front desk, see if anyone has made an initial report with them?"

"On it now, boss."

Sam paced the area, recapping the conversation she'd had with the killer, searching for a clue.

Bob joined her, pacing up and down the area. "Didn't you recognise his voice?"

"Do you think I'd be standing here, pacing, if I did?"

Her partner stopped walking. She reached the desk in front of her and returned to where he was standing, sulking.

"I'm sorry," she said, "but sometimes you can try the tolerance of a saint when you ask the dumbest of questions."

"I happen to think it's an important question, but hey, what do I know, me being a lowly DS?"

"Bob, give me a break. I can do without all this crap. Don't you think I have enough going on in my head already?"

"All right, can you stop snapping my head off now?" His shoulders sank, and he went back to his seat.

Sam debated whether to go over to him to apologise, but Oliver waved to gain her attention. She changed direction and crossed the room to speak with him. "Anything?"

"Yes, a man dropped in, reported his wife missing and was told to come back later today."

"Shit. You'd think someone down there would have the common sense... forget I said anything."

"Weekend staff, boss. Maybe they're not clued up about what's been going on this week."

"Maybe you're right. Okay, let me have the details. Bob and I will pay the husband a visit."

Oliver handed over a slip of paper, and Sam scanned the address.

"Come on, Bob, we've got work to do. Guys, keep going over the previous cases and looking into the criminals who have been recently released. Also, Liam, let's get a search warrant sorted for the gym to obtain all the members' details. We know he's a member there, let's see if we can use that information to nail this bastard. Can't stand him laughing at me, at us."

Bob joined her at the door, and they walked down the stairs together.

"Are you still in a bad mood?" she asked.

"Nope. All forgotten, I'm the utter professional."

She laughed and almost lost her footing on the penultimate step. Bob steadied her before the momentum carried her into the wall opposite.

"Thanks, you're my hero."

"When you want me to be. At other times… nope, I'm not going there."

Sam sniggered, and they sprinted out of the main entrance towards the car.

MR ROBERTS WAS A QUIVERING WRECK, wringing his hands as he spoke. "I've let her down. I told her to stay where she was while I fetched the car because the weather was foul and she only wore a flimsy dress with a matching jacket out that night."

"And at what time was this on Saturday, sir?"

"We ate early, at around seven, and she wanted to go home at about eight-thirty because she had one of her migraines starting up. Why didn't I insist on her coming with me? Because I never in my wildest dreams ever thought something like this would happen, not to her. She's a strong woman, she wouldn't fall for no daft sob story, so he must have whacked her over the head and dragged her into a waiting vehicle or something. That's what my mind has come up with, and believe me when I say this, I've thought long and hard, trying to work out why she went missing."

"Were there many people milling around, outside the restaurant?"

"No. It was surprisingly quiet for a Saturday." He glanced across the lounge to the handbag sitting on the small dining table tucked at one end of the room. "I found her bag on the steps. Her phone is inside, so there would be no point trying to contact her. It's all a mess, and what happens in my hour of need? I go down the cop shop, only to be told to come back once the first twenty-four hours are up! Seriously?

Even when someone is adamant their wife has been kidnapped? Is that really what it's come to nowadays? You lot dismissing a person's word with a flick of your wrist? My God, isn't there enough in the press these days about how shoddy police forces are right now? Look at the Met and all those crimes that have been committed against women lately. Jesus, if you can't trust the fucking police then who can you trust?"

"All I can do is apologise and put it down to a change of shift at the weekend. My team and I have been working on several similar cases in the past week. I have to tell you that we believe your wife was probably abducted by the same man."

"What? You know who this person is and he's still wandering the streets, or driving around out there, pouncing on further victims? And yet, when I report my wife missing, presumed taken, your lot don't want to know. Jesus Christ, this country is a frigging shambles. What with all the strikes going on, the state the force is in, as I've already stated. What hope do I have of getting Jean back alive?"

"Every hope. You have to remain positive. The last two women he abducted were found safe and well."

"How many women in total has he kidnapped?"

"Only two." Sam chewed on her lip.

His eyes narrowed. "I know there's more, what else aren't you telling me?"

She closed her eyes and braced herself for the torrent of abuse she anticipated coming her way. "We believe his first victim was left for dead in a park."

"Holy shit! So what you're telling me is that a possible killer has probably taken my wife."

"If it's the same man we've been dealing with, his MO appears to have changed recently. Therefore, I wouldn't consider that an option. I'm not. The man is in touch with me. He's keen on leading me and my team on treasure hunts to find the victims. I have every confidence that he will be in touch with me soon regarding your wife."

"But that's pure conjecture on your part. There are no guarantees, because he's already changed his MO once. What's to say he won't change it again where she's concerned? Fucking hell, how can you sit there so calmly and spout this shit?"

"I'm sorry you feel that way. I believed by revealing how he's played things in the past, it might go some way towards you having confidence in me and my team of bringing your wife home safely to you."

"You reckon? All you've succeeded in doing is making my mind work overtime. I have half a dozen scenarios bouncing around now instead of just the one I had before. How did you find the other women?"

"He sent me notes about their whereabouts in the form of riddles. My team and I managed to suss out the locations quickly."

"Thank God for that. And what state were the women in when you found them?"

"I'm not going to lie or try to pull the wool over your eyes. They were distressed but alive, that should be all that matters."

"And why did he kidnap these women? For what purpose...? Oh God, now I've said the words out loud, I really don't want to know the answer."

"It's best not to ask. I can't go into detail anyway, because the women have a right to their privacy."

"Jesus, I can guess without you laying it on a plate for me." His hands slid through his hair, and he rocked back and forth on the edge of the sofa. "Why didn't Jean come with me to the car? Why am I always being a gent with her? This time it backfired on both of us, big time." His hands dropped into his lap, and his gaze sought out Sam's. "I just want her back, unharmed. Can you help me, Inspector? Because if you can't, then I don't know who I can turn to for help."

"We're here and we're not going anywhere. All we can do is sit tight for now until he contacts us again. Judging by past experience, he will be in touch sooner rather than later."

"I hope you're right."

"We're going to need the name of the restaurant where the incident took place."

"The Happy Eater, it's in Alexander Street."

"We're going to pay them a visit, see if they have any CCTV on the premises. Are you going to be all right on your own? Maybe you should contact a member of your family or a friend and ask them to come and sit with you."

"No, I couldn't do that. I'm fine on my own. Yes, you must go, I've taken up enough of your time. You won't find this person, and my wife, sitting around here, talking with me, will you?"

"It was a necessary evil, to get all the facts straight. Try not to worry, please have faith in us as a team. Hopefully, we'll have you reunited with your wife soon."

He showed them to the door. "I'm sorry for being snarky with you, please forgive me, it was the frustration talking. I'm usually a very placid man, things don't normally faze me. But I don't mind admitting, I feel like a lost cause without Jean by my side and knowing that she is in the hands of this dangerous person."

Sam touched his forearm. "Please, I know it's easier said than done, but try not to worry."

"I have confidence in you, Inspector, aware of the two women you have saved already. Please don't let me down."

"We're going to do our very best, I assure you. Take care of yourself. I've got your number. I'll be in touch soon if I have any news for you."

CHAPTER 13

The staff at the restaurant were already on site, setting up for the lunchtime service. The manager opened the door to them in a pair of jeans and a T-shirt that had a rip in one of the sleeves. "Excuse the mess, I need to set up the bar in the morning, and that includes changing barrels of beer. My wife would go berserk if I changed them in my best work suit. Come in. How can I help? Mind if I continue to stock up the bar at the same time?"

"I'm not opposed to the idea at all," Sam said. "Thanks for making time to see us."

"What's this about?"

Don Cochran invited them to take a seat at the bar and then slid a crate of fruit juices over to the fridge.

Bob removed his notebook from his pocket and flipped it open on the bar.

"It's a delicate matter really. On Saturday evening, it would appear that a woman may have been abducted outside your restaurant."

"Are you sure? Sodding hell, I've never heard that before.

How do you know?" He stood, left the crate where it was and approached the bar.

"Her husband said he left her waiting on the steps. When he returned from fetching the car, his wife was missing, but her handbag was sitting on the top step outside your restaurant."

"Damn. Okay. So I take it you'll be wanting to view the footage from the cameras, right?"

"That would be great, if you wouldn't mind accommodating us."

"Jilly, can you get Max to finish off stocking up the fridge for me?"

"Yes, boss," a woman cleaning the tables shouted back.

Don led them through the restaurant and the kitchen at the rear and turned left into what could only be described as a disaster zone of an office. "I'd apologise, but there wouldn't be any use. We're understaffed, and something has to give around here. If I'm not out there in the restaurant all hours of the day and night, I'm helping out in the kitchen. Paperwork and keeping a tidy office aren't at the top of my list of priorities at the moment."

Sam smiled. "I totally understand. We're not here to judge you, I swear."

"Good. I feel bad that I've let it get in this state, it's going to be a mammoth task sorting it all out. Okay, excuses out of the way, let me try and clear a path to the equipment." He kicked a few empty boxes out of the way and knocked over a pile of leaflets. "Damn, yet more mess to clear up now. It's never-ending." After reaching the machine, he removed the disc for Sunday and slotted the Saturday one in its place. "What time?"

"Around eight-thirty, maybe a few minutes before."

He whizzed through the disc and stopped it at eight twenty-five.

Sam pointed and said, "That's them. He left her on the steps so she didn't get wet. He informed us that she was wearing a thin dress with a matching jacket. That much is true. This is where the husband leaves her. He set off, and bloody hell, this man approached his wife within seconds."

She watched the younger man peer over his shoulder several times. He seemed anxious, his intent obvious. Jean Roberts spoke with him and opened her mouth to scream. The man hit her in the face, hard enough to knock her out. The three of them winced after witnessing the impact.

"Ouch!" Bob said unnecessarily. "He's got some front, I'll give him that. To kidnap her right outside a busy restaurant."

"I find it incredibly hard to believe that no one saw the incident or reported it," Sam stated.

"You've seen it, the entrance is off to the side," Don said. "There are a lot of oak struts just inside, I suppose they would hamper anyone's view. There's also the fact that if people are here dining, they would be more than likely engrossed in their conversations. It's usually couples or group parties we cater for, we rarely entertain individuals clogging up a table on the busy night of the week."

"I get you," Sam said. "He dragged her down the steps, presumably to his waiting car, not that we've got a view of that. Do you have any other cameras outside, perhaps viewing a different angle?"

"I've got one down the side of the building that focuses on the staff entrance down there. It might be beneficial, let's see." He switched discs again, and the camera was trained on the door down an alley. "I'll speed through it to the right time. Here we are. Yes, there's a car at the top. Can't make out what it is, though, sorry. It's not going to get better than that."

Sam paused to think. "Wait, what about the property opposite?"

"Yes, Jack's place. He's got like a tapas bar across the road. I'm sure he mentioned he put a camera in last year after a bout of trouble involving some rowdy drinkers. I'll give him a call, if you want?"

"Thanks, that'd be great."

He withdrew his phone from the back pocket of his jeans and looked through his contacts. "Jack, it's Don. Sorry to trouble you, mate, I've got the police with me. They're enquiring about an incident that took place on Saturday night outside my gaff. We've managed to locate some of the footage, but I was wondering if your cameras might have picked up a car that was used in the incident." He raised a thumb at Sam. "Brilliant. I'm in the middle of setting up. Can I send them over to you...? Cheers, mate, I owe you one, again." He ended the call and smiled. "He said to join him in a few minutes, he's sure he'll have what you're looking for."

"That's great. I can't thank you enough. We'll leave you to get back to your work."

They left the restaurant and dodged their way through the heavy traffic to cross the road to Jack's Tapas Bar.

"Hey, are you the police?" a young man with an enthusiastic smile asked as soon as they entered the bar.

"We are. Is Jack around?" Sam showed her ID.

"He is. He told me to take you through to see him when you arrived. Come this way. The hallway is cluttered, we've not long had a delivery, and I'm in the process of getting the stock put away."

"You're fine. Thanks for the warning. Has this place been open long?"

"About two years. It was slow to start with, but since word got around, we get by. Weekends are busier than in the week."

"Like most places, I should imagine," Sam replied.

"I've been here with my wife, love the food," Bob said.

"She prefers eating smaller, what I call picky meals, rather than sit down to a full three courses somewhere. Me, I had to buy fish and chips on the way home."

Sam groaned inside. *Bob and his big mouth strikes again.* She nudged him with her elbow.

The young man saw it and laughed. "Don't worry, it's not to everyone's taste. We appreciate how healthy a British man's appetite can be."

"And some," Bob muttered. "I said the food was good, but it was a bit like going out for a Chinese. I'm always hungry after one of them as well."

"All right, partner, unless there are any other food chains you want to upset, I'd keep my mouth shut if I were you."

"Fact. Deal with it," he snapped back.

Sam narrowed her eyes, warning him to keep his trap shut or face disciplinary action when they got back to base.

"Jack, I've got Inspector Cobbs and her partner here to see you."

"Thanks, Miguel. I shouldn't be too long. Keep putting the stock away. I'll continue setting up the tables when I'm done here."

Miguel spun on his heel and left the room.

"This is really good of you to trawl through the discs for us," Sam said.

"It's no problem. Do you want me to leave you to it? It's all pretty straight forward."

"We're in kind of a rush, so I think it would be better if you guided us through the disc, if you don't mind?"

"Not at all. Glad to be of assistance. What have we got then?" He played the disc.

Sam and Bob eagerly watched on, delighted to get another view of the incident.

"That's the hubby going to fetch their car, and here's the

other guy making his move. He's pretty brazen, hasn't bothered trying to disguise himself at all," Bob observed.

"Can you pause it as soon as you get a good look at him, please?" Sam asked.

"Fair enough," Jack replied. He paused the disc a few seconds later. "How's that?"

"Looks perfect to me," Bob said. He faced Sam who was staring at the suspect with her mouth gaping open. "Sam, are you okay?"

She shook her head and gulped down the saliva filling her mouth. "Yes. Can we get a copy of that, and then can you move the frame on to see if you can pick up the number plate?" She slotted into professional mode, ignoring, or trying to ignore, her heart slamming rhythmically against her ribs.

Him! Shit! What was his name? Is it him? Jesus, I'm doubting myself now. Shit!

"Will this do? It gives you half the reg number, which is better than nothing at all," Jack said. His brow furrowed. "Are you all right? The colour has drained from your cheeks."

"I'm fine. Thanks for your concern. We really appreciate your help." She turned on her heel and dashed out of the confined office, back through the bar area and out into the street where she sucked in a few deep breaths to replace the stale air circulating her insides.

Bob caught up with her seconds later. "What the heck is going on? The only thing I can think of is that you know this fucker. Do you?"

"I think so. It's been years since I've seen him."

"How many years?"

Sam took off towards the car park.

Bob ran after her and gripped her arm. "What's going on? Why are you ignoring me?"

She wrenched her arm out of his grasp and marched the

extra ten feet to her car. "I'm not. My mind feels like a mini tornado is causing havoc up there. I'm trying to think and…"

"And?" he prompted.

"When he spoke to me on the phone earlier, he was hinting that he knew me. Why didn't I pick up on that then?"

"Stop blaming yourself. What good is it going to do you in the end?"

They continued to the car, and Sam pressed the key fob to unlock it. She slipped in behind the steering wheel and immediately jumped out of her seat again. Remembering to snap on a pair of gloves, she removed the envelope that had been secured under her windscreen wiper and returned to the car.

"Eyes like a hawk, you have. I missed it completely," her partner admitted.

"He was here. He could still be here… watching our every move. He's toying with me, with us, Bob."

"I'm not about to disagree with you. You read the note, and I'll keep my eyes open, see if I can spot anyone taking an interest in us."

"Don't forget his car, we know what make and model it is now."

"Don't worry, I hadn't. Open the damn note, Sam."

"Patience. I'm building up to it."

He heaved out an impatient sigh. "In your own time."

She carefully opened it and removed the note.

T IME, *if only we could go back in time, Sam.*

You and me, we were so in love once, weren't we? Or don't you remember?

You're infuriated, aren't you? I can tell. Yes, I've been watching you, keeping my eye on you for years, and it has come to this, me taking my revenge.

For what? I hear you ask.

For dumping me when I was consumed with love for you.

Back in the day, we used to be good together, until Chris came along.

Funny that. I thought once he was out of your life, you'd seek me out, come running back for forgiveness. How wrong was I?

Why commit the crimes I've been committing lately? That's what you're dying to know, isn't it? It's because I can, I wanted to punish you for not caring. I've punished these women because you didn't care enough to come back to me. To look me up in your hour of need.

Instead, you've moved on, like the slag you are and always were. You've always been the type of woman who needs a man in her life, you're useless without one. Go on, admit it.

You should have looked me up. We had something special back in the day, until the day you met Chris, then our whole relationship went downhill, didn't it? But I don't have to remind you of that, do I?

Anyway, what's the point in living in the past, some would say, and they'd be right, except I live with those memories in my head every day and find them impossible to shift. All too consuming, believe me.

Anyway, anyway... you'll be wanting to get your hands on the latest victim, won't you? She's where we shared our final picnic. Get that wrong, and her life will be lost. TTFN.

"Jesus Christ, it's him. I know who it is."

"Who? Are you going to let me read the note?" Bob had tried to get a sneaky read, but Sam had tilted the slip of paper away from his prying eyes.

"Put some gloves on first."

He did as instructed, and Sam handed the note over and observed his facial expressions alter while he read it.

"What the fuck! You dumped him back in the day and now he's seeking revenge?"

"That's pretty much what it amounts to, yes. I'm trying to recall where he lived."

"More importantly, do you remember his name?"

"That as well. I think it's either Peter or Phil."

"How many bloody boyfriends have you had over the years, or shouldn't I ask?"

"Not many. But it's not about that, Bob. We went out for a few months, but I didn't really feel an affinity towards him. If I had, my eye wouldn't have wandered, would it?"

"What a bloody mess. He's a mess! To seek revenge for something which took place eons ago."

"He must be. Let's get back to the station. We're all going to need to put our heads together."

"Don't give up just yet, remember we've got a partial on the plate. What you need to do is come up trumps with his name."

"Hey, believe me, I'm trying."

Sam started the car, and all the way to the exit, her gaze was glued to her rear-view mirror, on the lookout for anyone following them.

If he was out there, spying on them, he was doing a great job of remaining hidden, because neither she nor Bob spotted him.

BOB GATHERED the team around while Sam fixed them both a coffee upon their return. She ran through what she remembered about Pete or Phil, or whatever his name was, which amounted to very little, and then the map came out. Sam's mind wandered back to long ago, to the days when she had time on her hands to partake in a picnic here and there. She jotted down a few locations that sprang to mind and, as she recollected those times, everything appeared to slot into place. "I remember. He was called Philip Garner, I think. He lived somewhere over near High Harrington, or close to that area."

"And the picnic sites?" Bob asked then took a sip from his coffee.

"I'm still trying to recall them."

"I'll do a search for the name through the system," Claire said, aiming a sympathetic smile at Sam.

"Let's all get on it. I'll keep searching the map, hopefully something will come to mind." Sam reread the note to see if Garner had slipped any further clues in there to help her cause, but she shook her head over and over the more she read it.

"Are you okay?" Bob came to a standstill beside her and asked.

"I'm not sure is the honest answer. It's like he's punishing me all over again for not getting in touch with him after Chris's death."

"He's a weirdo."

"A dangerous weirdo who has killed and abducted innocent women, why? In an effort to get to me. To get noticed. Makes me wonder what his endgame is."

"You can't think about that, Sam. What you need to focus on is the locations. How many picnics did you guys go on together?"

She puffed out her cheeks and expelled the air in her lungs. "I think I need to grab some time alone, in my office, see what I can come up with."

"Sounds like an excellent idea to me."

Taking the map with her, Sam snuck into the office and spread the large sheet over her desk. "I refuse to let you get the better of me, you bastard."

She closed her eyes and drifted back to days gone by, to

when they'd been going out together, and shuddered. Suddenly, it all came back to her, the way he'd treated her, couldn't keep his hands off her. The swipes he'd taken at her arse as she'd walked by. It was one of those actions that really wound her up.

Yes, I can remember him well now. Such a bloody creep. I've successfully blocked him out of my mind all these years, and now I'm being forced to revisit that time. Where did we go?

She closed her eyes and was thrilled when a few images she had locked away in the little box at the back of her mind came surging back. Sam picked up a pen and circled a few areas. She could only recall going on a few picnics with him.

Were there more? Birthdays, his and mine? Did we really spend that much time together? I remember trekking across the fells with one guy in particular in my teens. Was that him?

Certain images came flooding back. She ended up circling three different areas. She returned to the incident room and spread out the map on the desk again. "I've come up with three possible locations."

"I've got his details from DVLA, boss," Claire was quick to add.

"Great news, Claire. We'll deal with that in a minute."

The team gathered around and studied the highlighted areas on the map.

"It's no good you telling us there could be three, he was very specific, asked you to remember your final picnic with him," Bob reminded her.

Sam glared at him. "What do you think I've been trying to do? I've come up with three locations, it's better than none at all."

"And what, you want us to trek out there and split up again, like we did last time?"

"It was successful then, there's no reason it shouldn't be a second time," Sam countered logically.

Bob perched on the desk behind him and folded his arms. Sam rolled her eyes at him.

"I think it's doable, boss. If we take enough uniformed officers with us," Liam interjected swiftly.

"My thoughts exactly, Liam." Her eye was drawn to one location on the map, and she pointed at it. "I've remembered. We tried to find the watermill at Borrowdale, it was off the beaten track. That has to be the place." She glanced at her watch. "At least we have daylight on our side this time, it's only two o'clock. I think it used to be called *The Secret Mill*."

"I know the place. My girlfriend and I discovered it a few years ago on one of our walks," Oliver told the team. "The terrain around there can be treacherous in parts."

"Something to be aware of. Why don't we all head out there now? It shouldn't take us too long to get there, to the car park," Sam suggested.

"It says on Google that the old water, or secret mill, can be found at Coombe Gill between Rosthwaite and Seatoller in Borrowdale," Bob chipped in after looking up the information on his phone.

"I'd say about forty-five minutes, boss," Liam said.

"Let's go. I'll see the desk sergeant on the way out."

The team gathered their jackets, all except Claire who was still busy typing away at her keyboard.

"I'll continue to dig, see what I can find out about Philip Garner, boss."

"Anything you feel I should know urgently, ring me, Claire. Come on, guys, time is running out for the current victim if he has that location in mind." Sam headed for the door.

She made a detour to the armoury along with Liam to pick up their Tasers. Then they retraced their steps and joined the others in the reception area.

"Must be something bad if you're all heading out," Nick said from behind the reception counter.

"We believe we know where the current victim is. Any chance your guys can lend a hand, Sergeant?"

"Tell me what you need, ma'am."

"At least two patrol cars, if not more. We're heading out to Borrowdale. To The Secret Mill out that way."

"I know the one. It's secret all right. I've known dozens of people give up while trying to find it. Lots of photographers get up that way."

"That's right, I remember the place being talked about by my father who is a keen photographer. We're going to make a move, if your men can catch us up, Nick."

"You carry on, they won't be far behind you, don't worry."

Sam smiled and pushed through the main door. Bob jumped in the car next to her, and Suzanna joined them in the back seat. The other three male members of the team hopped into Liam's car.

NERVES WERE GETTING the better of Sam on the journey. She got far too close to the car in front at one point and when the driver braked and indicated to turn right, she almost rammed him up the arse.

"Steady, keep your eyes on the road, boss, otherwise we'll be getting there via the hospital."

Sam pulled a face at Bob. "Is that the sign up ahead?"

"That's it. It's the nearest car park to the location."

All around them lay breath-taking peaks and valleys.

"Stunning," Suzanna sighed.

"This whole area is amazing. Have you ever walked up here, Suzanna?"

"No, boss, it's definitely on my to-do list for the near future."

"Can we stop the chit-chat and get on with it?" an impatient Bob asked.

"Okay, keep your Y-fronts on, if you wear them," Sam replied.

The retort had Bob fuming but made Suzanna chuckle.

The three of them exited the car and joined the others close to the start of the footpath which led through a small wooded area.

"Is it far now?" Bob asked.

"Around thirty minutes if my memory serves me right," Sam said, unsure.

"Well, your memory hasn't really been up to scratch lately, has it?" Bob whispered for her ears only.

"Screw you, buster. I've done my best. How was I to know this was all about an incident that had happened in my past?"

"A bit of logical thinking might have helped. It wasn't until I suggested this could be to do with you a few days ago… if I hadn't aired my views, we'd be none the wiser now until he sent that last note."

"All right, you don't need to keep rubbing it in."

"To the right, ma'am." Oliver pointed at the craggy boulders over that way.

"Looks good. Here we go, folks. Liam, you should stick with me. We both need to be alert, ready to take aim if it's needed."

"Why? Do you think he's going to be here?" Bob asked.

"Not sure. I'm just being more cautious than usual, given what this guy has put the other victims through."

They rounded the boulders, and the watermill made a spectacular appearance in front of them. The sound of the surging, running water drew Sam's attention first.

Suzanna gasped and pointed at an area near another cluster of boulders. A red piece of material could be seen bobbing near the rocks by the river. "Is that her?"

"She was wearing an outfit that colour when she was abducted, so there's every chance it's her."

The closer they got to the river, the more thunderous the noise became.

"It's not her," Bob shouted. "It's just her dress by the looks of it."

Sam scanned the area close to the mill and strained her ear and heard a woman scream. "Over there. That's them."

Two figures, one fully-clothed and the other half-naked, were running away from the area.

"He's obviously seen us. Where could they be heading?" Suzanna asked.

"Up towards the fell is my guess. Come on, we need to get to them," Sam shouted above the din of the torrential water.

"We're going to need to go back. We can't go over the rocks, they're covered in thick moss, we'll be endangering our lives," Bob said.

Sam nodded her agreement, and the six of them quickly retraced their steps and took the other route around the mill. She stopped to peer ahead of them, unsure which direction to take when the footpath divided into two.

"Uh-oh, I know what's coming next." Bob groaned.

Sam jabbed him in the side with her elbow. "Liam, Oliver and Alex, you go right, we'll go left. Liam, keep your Taser drawn, ready to use. Don't hesitate to shoot if you fear the woman's life is in immediate danger."

"Yes, boss."

The group split up. Sam led the way to the right, her ear cocked at all times, and her gaze scanning the terrain all around them.

"Nothing," Bob shouted, ever the pessimist.

"Give it a chance, partner."

Suzanna was the first to spot movement over to their right. She tapped Sam on the back and pointed.

"Got it."

The woman screamed again and forced them to up their pace.

"Bob, get on the phone to Liam, tell them to get over here," Sam said.

Bob paused to make the call while Sam and Suzanna forged on ahead.

"No… I won't let you take me… No… I won't," the woman shouted.

Sam trotted to get closer. Garner and Jean Roberts were hiding behind a boulder. Sam could just make out the tops of their heads.

"We need to get closer without alerting them," Sam whispered.

Suzanna pointed out a grassy path over to their right. "The grass will deaden our footsteps. The ground this way is too uneven, and the gravel will make a noise underfoot."

"You're right. Come on."

They managed to get to within a few feet of the boulder when they heard the man cry out and curse the woman. Sam ran ahead, rounded the boulder and, with her Taser drawn, confronted Garner.

"Hello again, Phil. Long time no see."

"Help me," Jean Roberts pleaded.

"It's okay, Jean, you're safe now. This has all been a grave misunderstanding, hasn't it, Phil?"

"Has it? I don't think so. If you think you've got the upper hand over me just because you're holding the Taser, Sam, you're an idiot to believe that." He produced a knife from up his sleeve and placed it against Jean's throat.

Sam glanced down to see Jean had a rock in her hand. Phil kept his gaze trained on Sam. An uncomfortable expression appeared on his face as his gaze travelled the length and breadth of her body.

"You can't get away from me, Garner. I have my whole team in the area. Give up the knife, and we'll go back to the station and have a chat about what you've been up to for the past seven days."

"Stop telling me what to do, Sam. I never appreciated it when we were together."

"I can't even remember what it was like back then. Remind me?" she asked, deliberately keeping him distracted. Out of the corner of her eye, she could see the other team had arrived and that Liam was using his initiative and getting into position on the other side of the boulder. Maybe he'd be able to catch Garner off-guard and fire his Taser.

"Typical. Everything is all about you, it always was, wasn't it, Sam?"

She shook her head. "I don't recall it being that way, Garner. Now put the knife down before someone gets hurt."

He laughed and purposefully nicked Jean's throat with the blade. She yelped. Held Sam's gaze for a few seconds and mouthed, "One, two..." On three, Jean attacked Garner with the rock, and Sam squeezed the trigger. Garner made a dramatic dive to his right. Jean took her opportunity to get clear of her abductor. Oliver gathered her in his arms and wrapped a blanket around her shoulders.

Sam released the trigger, and Bob and Alex secured Garner with the cuffs. The wires were removed and he was pulled to his feet by Alex, and together they marched him back to the waiting vehicles. He was put in the back of one of the patrol cars and driven off.

Sam high-fived her team on another job well done, and they drove Jean to the hospital to be checked over. Bob called her husband on the way, and he joined them not long after they arrived.

"I can't thank you enough for bringing her back to me

safely," Paul Roberts said. He threw an arm around his wife's shoulders and pulled her close.

"Yes, thank you, Inspector," Jean said.

"Hey, you played your part. If it hadn't been for your bravery... well, the outcome might have been totally different. I'm glad we found you. Take care, both of you."

Sam drove back to the station. The team celebrated their success at the Red Lion pub across the road, and then she headed home for the night, choosing to interview Garner after he'd suffered a night in the cells.

EPILOGUE

Refreshed, after spending a lovely evening with Rhys and the dogs, a rejuvenated Sam headed back into the station the next morning.

According to the desk sergeant Garner had spent a restless night in his cell.

Sam took her time, making sure her preparations were all in order for the interview. She received the call from Nick that the duty solicitor had arrived and then she and Bob made their way down the stairs and into Interview Room One to tackle her ex.

Bob said the necessary verbiage for the recording, and Sam asked her first question.

"Why, Philip? Why come after me after all these years?"

"Because I could."

"Why involve other women in your evil game?"

"Because I could."

Bastard. Instead of going down the 'no comment' route, he's going to tout 'because I could'.

The interview lasted another thirty minutes and

consisted of Sam asking questions and Garner replying with the same response. Sam called the interview to a halt.

As she left the room, Phil shouted, "You should have contacted me, begged for my forgiveness."

Sam returned to the desk and leaned over the table. "In your dreams, arsehole." Then she walked out of the room.

Bob applauded her all the way up the stairs. "Go you," he said over and over.

The team worked hard the following couple of days, getting all the paperwork up to scratch. Sam booked a few days off from work and arranged for Rhys to do the same.

When Friday morning came around, she announced they were going away.

"We are? Where are we going?" Rhys asked.

She slipped into his outstretched arms. "It's a surprise. I need some time with the men in my life."

"Sounds good to me. Just one thing."

Sam tilted her head and asked, "What's that?"

"Are you sure there are no other crazy exes in your past who are likely to show up in the future?"

"God, I hope not. Time will tell, I suppose." She smirked.

They shared a kiss that rippled to the tip of her toes.

THE END

THANK you for reading To Control Them the next thrilling adventure **To Hold Responsible**

. . .

HAVE you read any of my fast paced other crime thrillers yet? Why not try the first book in the DI Sara Ramsey series <u>No Right to Kill</u>

OR GRAB the first book in the bestselling, award-winning, Justice series here, <u>Cruel Justice.</u>

OR THE FIRST book in the spin-off Justice Again series, <u>Gone In Seconds.</u>

PERHAPS YOU'D PREFER to try one of my other police procedural series, the DI Kayli Bright series which begins with <u>The Missing Children.</u>

OR MAYBE YOU'D enjoy the DI Sally Parker series set in Norfolk, <u>Wrong Place.</u>

OR MY GRITTY police procedural starring DI Nelson set in Manchester, <u>Torn Apart.</u>

OR MAYBE YOU'D like to try one of my successful psychological thrillers <u>She's Gone</u>, <u>I KNOW THE TRUTH</u> or <u>Shattered Lives.</u>

KEEP IN TOUCH WITH M A COMLEY

Pick up a FREE novella by signing up to my newsletter today.
https://BookHip.com/WBRTGW

BookBub
www.bookbub.com/authors/m-a-comley

Blog

http://melcomley.blogspot.com

Why not join my special Facebook group to take part in monthly giveaways.

Readers' Group

Printed in Great Britain
by Amazon